I0592778

Dedication

to Judy Otterson

The Body in the Truck

Tim Kern

TIM KERN

The Body in the Truck

FIRST EDITION

MYSTERY ONE™ Publications

The Body in the Truck

FIRST EDITION

The Body in the Truck

Tim Kern

<u>Acknowledgments</u>

Many thanks are extended to the readers of my
earlier books, who encouraged me to keep
writing, always in hope that
the next book would be better.

To fellow novelist and friend, Claudia Pfeiffer,
and to C.M., whose encouragement and
critical eye made this tale readable.

The Body in the Truck

Tim Kern

Contents

Chapter One:
You're gonna need a different truck.

Sunday, May 27, 2018; near Michigan City, Indiana, USA: "Okay, Mr. Terwilliger. You're all set. Let's go out and get your truck," said Gino Sabbatini, the manager at U–Drive–Em Truck Rental. "Here's your dolly and ten moving blankets. Wait here. I'll go get your twenty–footer."

Gino, thirty–four, had been working at U–Drive–Em for a dozen years. His customer service and cheerful attitude, along with a deep interest in how businesses worked and his attention to making people happy, had gotten him promoted at every opportunity; now he was managing the show for Vittorio Tonelli, who was, for all practical purposes, retired. Tonelli came into the shop on Gino's days off and maybe twice a month besides, to check the books, which were his daughter Alfetta's job. Alfetta was forty–five and thought Gino was cute.

On this brilliant Sunday morning in May, Josh Terwilliger was moving to Socorro, Texas, a place he'd found on the Internet but never visited, right near El Paso, Texas. He hoped to find work on President Trump's Wall. Socorro—the area, anyway—was small but booming, and home to five women for every four men; Josh figured he wouldn't mind the demographic advantage. Plus, housing was cheap, and he wouldn't miss the frigid winters of Indiana.

Gino brought the truck around front, crunching white gravel and kicking up a tiny bit of dust. Josh was waiting with the dolly and the blankets. Gino said, "Okay, I'm sure you know all this stuff, but let me just show you some of the safety features and the other things you should know about this truck. You ever drive something this big?"

Josh admitted he hadn't by saying it had been a while, so Gino walked him around the vehicle, explaining that right turns were the toughest ("You can scrape the side off this thing on a phone pole if you're not paying attention") and that the truck was tall enough to take out some gas–pump overheads. Inside the cab, he showed Josh where the emergency triangles and flares were and the phone numbers in the glove box, "so you can call us if you have a problem, which you won't have. But we've got roadside assistance twenty–four–seven, just in case."

At the back of the truck, Gino showed Josh how to pull out the ramp, stow it, and lock it. And he then asked, "Mr. Terwilliger, do you have a padlock for the overhead door? We have those— ten bucks, kind of expensive—but I'd recommend you get one, even if you don't want ours. Your stuff can disappear in a flash, while you're just chomping on a Big Mac." Josh pulled a padlock out of his jacket pocket. Gino nodded. "Now, let's see if you can get the door open."

Josh flipped the latch, lifted the handle about six inches, and the door was stuck. "Here," Gino said, "let me show you a trick." He gave a tiny push in the right spot, and the door ran itself to the top. It smelled dank inside.

Gino noticed the license plate on the floor. He leaned back, looked over the rear bumper where it was supposed to be. *What's it doing here?* And he leaned it against the side of the truck.

Gino clambered in and said, "Here, hand me the dolly and those blankets. I'll tie them to the side, so you can at least drive home with this open, get some of this funky smell out. Usually, though, don't drive anywhere with the door open, even partway open." Terwilliger nodded.

Gino's eyes adjusted to the dark interior, and for the first time, he looked all the way forward in the box, to the corner of the "dance floor" above the cab, where there was a black trash bag. "Oh— here's the problem," he said. "Somebody didn't clean this out all the way." Josh just smiled, and Gino continued, "Now I gotta go kick somebody's butt," and he walked to the front of the box and grabbed the bag. "This thing's heavy," he said. "Can you give me a hand?" He smiled apologetically. "I know it's not your job, but I don't want to dump garbage all over your nice new truck."

The brilliant sunlight outside made it doubly–hard to see inside the truck, especially way up front in the corner of the dance floor, but since the bag was the only thing in there, it was easy to find, even though getting a decent look at a black bag in a dark truck made it difficult to see any detail.

But as they dragged it to the edge of the dance floor, they felt that they ripped a hole in the bag, and just as they rolled it to the floor, the bag ripped wide open and the smell nearly knocked them over. Both men ran to the clean air at the back of the truck. "That is *awful*," Josh said.

"Yeah, I'm going to get you a new truck," Gino said, and they both hopped down to the gravel, gagging.

* * *

Back in the office, filling out paperwork for a different truck, Gino said, "Mr. Terwilliger, I'm really sorry about this." Then he opened the door to the shop and called out, "Hey, Eli! Can you get our customer another twenty? There's blankets and his dolly out front in the other truck. Get him ready, then go get that other one cleaned out. There's a mess of garbage in there. And let it air out; don't shut that door." As Eli brushed by on the way to the lot, Gino added, *sotto voce*, "and I want to talk with you as soon as you're done."

Josh Terwilliger finished the paperwork while Eli got the blankets and dolly transferred, and then he was on his way to Texas. Eli came into the office, the first truck still out front, back door open. "Gino…" he started to say. "Eli, I thought you had this one ready to go. Did you skip something? You know how embarrassing it is to open a truck full of trash and then have to ask the customer to help clean it out?"

"Gino, I'm trying to tell you," Eli stammered.

"Tell me what?"

"That's not garbage." Eli looked sick. His voice shook. "There's a body in that truck."

Gino stopped, looked at the truck. "A *what?* A body? You're sure?"

"I know what a hand looks like, and there's a hand sticking out."

Gino said, "Okay. Ummm… just pull the door shut; I'll call 911. Oh, crap."

* * *

In fifteen minutes, the first city squad car arrived. Gino met the patrolman at the door. "That's the truck?" he asked, and Gino nodded. "We'll just wait here a minute, until the crime scene guys get here."

"Want some coffee? A Pepsi?" Gino asked. The cop shook his head, then walked to the back door of the truck. And they waited another five minutes.

Two techs arrived in the Evidence Van, followed by the car of Detective Fred Stumpf, who sent the patrolman back to his regular work with a quick thank you.

Gino introduced himself, asked if they'd like him to open the truck, and they said they'd take it from here, and had anybody else been in the truck.

"Just me, the customer, and Eli," he said, and Stumpf asked him to go inside, and tell Eli to stick around.

Gino walked back into the shop and didn't see Eli. He went out back, to the parking lot, and found the skinny nineteen–year–old at the edge of the gravel, on his knees, throwing up into the weeds. Eli looked up. He looked pitiful. "I cleaned that truck real good when it came in," he said. "It's all swept and ready to go. There wasn't nothing in it. Nothing. I'd of seen it."

Gino squatted down next to him. "What about the license plate?" Eli shook his head.

"There was no plate in there. I don't remember checking if it was on the truck, but it for sure wasn't in there. I swept it out good."

"Don't worry about it, Eli. I know you wouldn't have missed a bag in there. But that's not a problem. We have a real problem on our hands. I mean, we have a friggin' dead body in one of our trucks!" He paused, patted Eli on the back as they both stood up. "Come on inside," he said. "Get yourself cleaned up, and let's see what the police want. Pepsi?"

Eli managed a faint smile. "Mountain Dew? Thanks." And he went into the men's room as Gino went to the front lobby and put dollar bills into the vending machine.

Detective Stumpf, short, stocky, rumpled–looking in spite of his suit, came in. He looked irritated as he ran his hand through his hair. Stumpf is one of those guys who, no matter how hard he tries, how shiny his shoes are, how clean his shirt—always looks scruffy. Stumpf seemed in a hurry as he said, "I'm going to need the records on that truck——who rented it last, when it went out, came in, where it came from, whatever you've got." Gino nodded. "And do you have cameras here, on the parking lot, especially?"

"We have two cameras inside," Gino said, "and two more outside, one in the front and one in the back, but the one out back stopped working. We should have a week's worth of all three cameras."

"Let's see 'em," the detective said. "Please."

Gino went around the corner into the tiny one—man office and returned with seven USB sticks, each labeled for a day of the week, and he laid them on the countertop. "This is our archive, officer," he said.

"Detective," said Stumpf.

"Sorry. Detective. But I want to say up front that these aren't going to be right. You can see, we have one for every day. We change them before we lock up. But the one that was in there right now says THURSDAY, and today is Sunday, so I don't know what's going to be on them."

Stumpf's usually grumpy expression turned grumpier. "That's not good. How many hours fit on each of these sticks?"

"I don't know," Gino said, "but more than twenty–four hours. All three cameras—all four, when they're working—they all go on one stick. So maybe—and I don't know this, either—maybe a stick holds more, if there's only three cameras working."

"Let's hope," said Stumpf. "Are you recording now?"

"Uhhh, no," Gino stumbled. "I'd better go put the spare stick in."

"Yeah, you'd better," Stumpf said, as he put the seven USBs into a plastic EVIDENCE baggie. Gino came back in a moment and Stumpf asked, "Aren't you running this place? Who's in charge of changing these thumb drives?"

Gino said, "I am, yeah. But I had Friday off. Either it was Mr. Tonelli, he's the owner; or his daughter, Alfetta."

Stumpf made notes in a little spiral–bound book. "Are you the one, left Thursday night, didn't change the stick for Friday?"

Gino felt sick. "I—I must have been thinking about my days off. Yeah, that's my job."

"Do you remember changing the stick before you went home?"

"I don't remember ever *not* doing it," Gino stumbled, "but I suppose it's possible. I just don't remember, specifically, if I changed the USB that night. I always do. It's automatic…"

"So you can't say whether you for sure did, or whether you maybe didn't change the sticks that night?"

Gino was frantic on the inside. *I don't remember doing it, but I never forget to do it. Come on, brain—help me out, here!* After a pause, during which the detective never took his eyes off him, he said, "I really can't tell you on a stack of bibles that I changed it," he said, "but I can tell you I don't remember ever *not* doing it. That's the most certain thing I can say. I'm… sorry."

Stumpf made another note. "So, let's get the paperwork on the last customer who rented this truck, and on the guy who rented it this time, okay?"

"That, I can do," Gino said, and he logged into the terminal. As the printer spat out sheet after sheet, Gino walked them to Stumpf.

The detective said, "So this truck came in on Tuesday. Have you had any other trucks, vans, trailers—whatever you rent here with wheels on it—any other rentals come in or go out since this truck arrived?"

Eli came into the office, said thanks for the Mountain Dew and he was going out to the shop to sit down a minute.

"Yes, sure, Detective," Gino said.

"Then I'll need everything you've got on those, too," Stumpf said.

I hope I don't run out of toner. Then Gino said. "Hey, uh, Detective, I thought of something. Eli cleaned that truck out on Thursday morning. We were running behind on maintenance. Eli had some shop work to do. So that body wasn't in there until after he cleaned it out—some time after, uh, ten. Eleven maybe, on Thursday morning. And the plate was definitely not on the floor of the box."

"If he's telling the truth, " Stumpf said. "And if your memory is right. Just, can you get me all the records, please?"

The printer kept whirring. "Okay," Gino said. "Here's everything. A van, another truck, and a car dolly. And the truck we just rented to Mr. Terwilliger. You already have the records on this truck."

"Thanks," Stumpf said, and he took the USBs, his notepad, and the stack of paperwork out to his car. Gino watched him as he emptied his pockets and hands into the car and then turned to the techs.

Gino got on the phone and called Vittorio Tonelli. Nobody answered. He left a message: "Vittorio, you need to call me right away. Everything's okay at the shop. I mean, everything's not okay. I mean, nothing is broken; nobody had an accident or anything. But it's serious. It's really really important that you call me right away. I can't leave details on your voicemail. Call me. Please."

Then Gino called Alfetta, left a note in her voicemail, just like the one he left for her father. He didn't notice Eli outside, remounting the license plate.

* * *

"What've you got?" Stumpf asked the first tech he saw.

Evidence Tech Keneesha Wright answered, "We have a black female, about thirty. Dark brown hair, about a hundred and thirty pounds—that's just our best guess on the age and weight. She's not wearing a ring or other jewelry that we saw."

"How long's she been in there?"

"Not very long, would be my guess. A day? She's cool from the night, though. We need to get her to the lab."

"Did you get all the pictures, prints you'll need?"

"Yes, sir. There may be some more prints on the plastic bag, but there's nothing good on the truck. We got pictures of the elevated section where she was resting, and also of the drag marks and how we found her, on the main floor. Plus pictures of getting the bag and her body onto the cart. We didn't lay her out. She's still more or less how we found her, in the fetal position."

"We didn't see anything particular," Keneesha continued, "but we didn't open the bag all the way. We're trying to keep everything the way we found it." Stumpf nodded.

"Anything to identify her?" Stumpf asked. "Jewelry, a purse, telephone?"

"Not that I saw. Whatever was in the bag is all there was. And whatever was in the bag, it's still in the bag. The truck is completely empty."

The other tech, a young woman named Tammy, said, "Sir?"

"Go ahead," said Stumpf.

"I think her skull might be broken in the back. It didn't feel right. I didn't look, but that's what it felt like to me."

"Thanks," he said. "Let's get her to the lab." They wheeled the cart to the van, mostly lifting it because it didn't navigate the gravel parking lot on its small wheels. And the body was off to the morgue.

Detective Stumpf climbed into the truck, turned on his flashlight. It had an ultraviolet beam as well as the normal white light. He closed the door until it was open just half a foot, and walked to the front of the van, gagging on the smell and shining the UV beam around.

The van, under UV light, was a mess. There were stains everywhere on the floor, drip marks on all the walls and the inside of the door, a few on the ceiling. The truck had been around the block as they say, and there were all sorts of stains. The dance floor had a fresh–looking spot on it where Eli said the bag had been, and smeared stains to its edge, then another spot on the floor, where he assumed Gino and Terwilliger had dropped it. But no bloody footprints that he could see. He called for another tech team. "And bring all the photo equipment you've got – IR, UV, all that fancy stuff," he added.

As Stumpf walked to the back of the truck, someone closed the door and he heard the latch snap shut. "Hey," he yelled, and he pounded on the door. "I'm still in here!"

The door opened and a sheepish Eli peered in. "Sorry, sir," he said. "I was just going to park the truck."

"Thanks," Stumpf said, as he jumped down onto the gravel. "No problem. But do not move this truck. Don't go back into it. Don't even touch it. I've got more guys coming." Eli nodded. "Do you mind showing me where it was parked the past couple days? Exactly?"

* * *

In the office, the phone rang. "U–Drive–Em, Gino speaking. How can I help you?" He was glad to have something normal distract him from the mess he was in. Or so he thought.

"What the hell is so important, Gino? Is everybody okay?" It was Tonelli.

"Hi, uh, Vittorio. Can you come to the shop? I'd rather tell you in person."

"Spit it out, Gino. I'm a busy man."

Yeah, that retirement must be killing you. "Okay. Well,…"

"Well, what?" *Tonelli must be drinking. Must have started early today. He's roaring mad, impatient. Unusual that he'd be so mean, or so early in the day.*

"Okay, Vittorio. Here it is: they found a body in a truck."

"What do you mean, '*They* found a body?' *Who* found a body? In one of our trucks? When?"

"Vittorio, please. Just… I had Eli bring a twenty–footer around front and we were putting the dolly and the blankets in, and there was a bag of—I thought it was garbage, but there was a body in it. The police are all over the place. I gave them the camera records."

"The cops are already there? Why didn't you call me first?"

"I—I just called 911 right away. Then I was answering questions. As soon as they took the body away, I called you."

There was silence from the other end. Vittorio finally said, "Don't go anywhere. I'll be there in half an hour. Tell them I'm on my way." And Vittorio hung up, told his home health worker to put her clothes back on and go home. Then he got in the shower, shaved, gargled some mouthwash and drove the ten minutes to U–Drive–Em.

* * *

Stumpf made a few more notes in his little spiral book, then went inside and waited until Gino was through with a customer who was returning a rented car dolly. "Gino," he said when the customer had left, "Can you get Alfetta down here for me to talk to, please? And in the meantime, can I see her personnel file?"

"Sure, Off... Detective," he said, "but she doesn't have a personnel file. She's Vittorio's daughter. I already called her, left a message."

"You 'left a message' hours ago. Doesn't she have a cell phone or something?"

"I called her cell. I don't know if she even has a land line. Anyway, no; she hasn't called back, and I've called her three times."

"Well, her name and phone, email, address—whatever you can give me, then. You do the payroll? Her Social Security number, age..."

"I do payroll, but Vittorio handles everything for Alfetta. I do have her email and phone number... Here," and he handed Stumpf a sheet of note paper with the U–Drive–Em logo on top. He wrote, "Alfetta Tonelli, alfettat@hotshot.com, 317–101–5999."

"That's all you have? How old is she? Date of birth? Do you have a copy of her driver's license? Do you know where she lives?"

"No. Sorry. She lives over in Stone Lake someplace; I was there once, but I can't say I could ever recognize it again. She's like, middle forties? She drives a silver Miata, a couple years old, if that's any help. Like I said, she's kinda special. Vittorio takes care of Alfetta himself."

"So, can you get her in here? Like, now?" Gino shrugged, about to remind the detective he had already called her, but Stumpf reasserted his authority. He said, "Call her again."

Gino dialed. "Hi, Alfetta," he said to her voice-mail. "You probably already know about the problem here. Detective Stumpf," he grabbed the card Stumpf held out to him, "657–3881. He's here now, so get in here as soon as you can, okay?" He ended the call, then said, "I'm going to text her, same message."

"Thanks. I'm going back to the station. Keep after her to call me. If I don't hear from her really soon, I'll send a SWAT team to go pick her up." He was lying, but it was worth the expression on Gino's face.

"Count on it, Officer."

"Detective."

"Detective. Yeah, sorry."

Stumpf was getting out of his car, back at the station, when his phone rang. "Hello, Detective Stump? This is Alfetta Tonelli. Gino said you had to talk to me right away."

"Stumpf, with an 'f.' Yes. You probably heard all about the body in one of your trucks… Yes, I would… Yes, at the Main Street Police Station…

Stumpf, Detective Stumpf. Just ask for me when you get here... No, just bring yourself."

Alfetta arrived in twenty minutes. "Have a seat," Stumpf said, as he led her into the break room. "Coke, water, coffee?"

"Water, thank you. What happened, Officer?"

"Detective. Well, suppose you tell me what you already know." Stumpf didn't like surprises, and he liked to keep a few cards up his sleeve during interviews, as much as he like seeing all of Alfetta's cards on the table.

"I heard they found a body in one of our trucks this morning. Nobody knows who it is, er, was, or why it was in there, or when it showed up. That's pretty much all I know."

"When did you find out?"

"Daddy—Vittorio Tonelli—he called me, told me on his way to the store, while he was driving."

"Did you get Gino's messages? He called you twice, maybe three times, got voicemail. And your father, he didn't tell you to come to the store? He didn't ask if you knew anything about it?"

"No. He just... just what I said. Told me he was heading to the store. Gino... I saw the messages as soon as I hung up with Daddy. I figured that was what he was going to tell me."

"He didn't tell you to get over here? You weren't curious? Did you talk to anybody else?"

"No. I figured Daddy had everything handled. And I didn't talk to anybody else. Well, not until I got Gino's messages all at once and called him back, just before I called you."

"You didn't think to come to the store? ...Okay. Let's get to this. Tell me where you've been since Thursday night, say, eight o'clock."

Stumpf took out his little notebook and Alfetta went through her days and nights, right up to when she listened to Gino's messages, after she talked with Vittorio.

Stumpf got up, said, "Stay there a minute," and walked into Redding's office.

Redding looked up. "How's she doing?"

"She's ready for you," Stumpf replied, and Jerry Redding put on his sport coat, straightened his tie, and grabbed his yellow pad. Stumpf slipped him the little notebook, open to the last page of their interview.

Alfetta was rattled. She kept crossing and recrossing her legs, her tight designer jeans as uncomfortable as they were stylish. Like her red stilettoes. Redding noticed she seemed uncomfortable in her near-shear white boat-neck top; she kept pulling her leather vest closed. There was no way to keep it closed, so she just kept fidgeting. And she smelled good. *Must have a quart of whatever she's wearing in that thousand-dollar rucksack she's carrying for a purse.*

Redding didn't know which of them was more distracted by her wardrobe. And her face–thin, smooth, and surrounded by long wavy black hair and set off, when she smiled, by perfect, brilliant teeth against a natural tan. *She could distract a monk.*

Redding focused on what he was about to ask. "Hello, Alfetta," he said. "I'm Detective Jerry Redding, and I have just a few questions for you, if you don't mind."

She was confused, but said, "Sure. Okay."

"So, Alfetta, you run the U–Drive–Em when Gino's not there? And you run it on most weekends, too?"

"Yes, that's right," she said.

"I know you've probably been all through this with Detective Stumpf, but I have just a few questions I'd like to ask, too." She shrugged. "First, though, can you tell me if all the cameras were working all the time since, say, Thursday night, midnight?"

"Yes, as far as I remember."

"And you changed out the USB stick in the security system each night when you closed?"

"Yes."

Vittorio said he closed, both nights. "And the cameras were working—all of them, both nights? Did you happen to look at them during the days, too?"

"Well, I'm sure they were working fine. I don't remember if I looked at them during the days. They're not very entertaining, you know."

"Fair enough. Now, will you tell me everything you did between last Thursday night and now? Starting with now and going backwards?" And Redding put the big yellow pad on the table, laid his pen down next to it, and looked into her eyes.

"I... I just did that for the other guy," she said. "Then you'll remember it that much easier for me," said Redding.

Alfetta stumbled, trying to remember what she had told Stumpf, occasionally making corrections as she thought through the sequence in reverse. Each time she relayed a fact, Redding wrote it down and said, "Now, you're sure of that?" or something else to rattle her. It worked; Alfetta spent twenty minutes telling Redding what she had told Stumpf in ten.

She corrected what she had said earlier three or four times, and said, "I'm not totally sure of exactly whether I did that first," a few times.

"That's okay," he'd say, then "but I'm really interested in whom you talked to—inside or outside of work, and when, and about what."

She spent another half an hour, starting with Gino's voicemails. Redding wrote everything down. "Well, thank you, Miss Tonelli. If you think of anything you left out, you have Detective Stumpf's card, right? And if we need to talk with you—you gave all your information to Connie, right?" She nodded yes to both questions and stood up. "Much obliged, Miss Tonelli."

Redding was surprised to see how tiny she was when she stood up. Even in those heels, she wasn't more than five-three. *Maybe the hair makes her look bigger.* As she passed by him and headed toward Connie's smiling self, Redding took another look. *Slim, but a real nice shape.* "Thank you, Miss Tonelli," he said. She didn't look back.

Redding went into Stumpf's office, took off his coat, loosened his tie. "She's lying," he said.

"Thought so," Stumpf said. "But about what?"

"Did you notice she didn't ask us any questions at all? 'Who's the victim?' 'When did they find him, or her? ' 'What happened to her?' all that?"

"Yeah," Stumpf said. "She was more concerned about getting her story just right than about anybody at the shop, or even the poor girl who spent the night in a plastic bag in the truck with her head near broke off. She smells."

"Who's next?" Redding asked. "You like Vittorio?"

"Vittorio's a trip. I think he pays less attention to the business than he does to his toenails, but he's really interested in this. Not every day he gets a dead one in his truck."

"At least, not one he doesn't already know," joked Redding. "Okay, let's talk to Vittorio."

"Hey, uhhh, Jerry? This is my case."

"Wanna trade? Mine's boring as hell."

Eli and Stumpf had just come in from the parking lot. Gino looked up and saw Vittorio's car pulling in. "That's the owner," he said to Stumpf, who turned and went out the door to meet him. The county's big Crime Scene Investigation Unit truck pulled in, immediately behind. Vittorio got out of his Lincoln and walked up to Stumpf, who ordered, "Just wait right here. I have to talk to them."

Tonelli, stunned and speechless, complied.

The detective walked to the truck, gave the techs some instructions. The team walked to the truck, opened the overhead door, and started taking pictures.

Vittorio said, "Hey! What are you doing?"

Stumpf looked at him, wanted to calm him down. "Mr. Tonelli, I presume? Detective Fred Stumpf. Do you have a few minutes to talk with me?" He motioned Vittorio inside. There, he looked at Gino and Eli. "Can we have some privacy, gentlemen?" The younger men left.

"What's going on? I get a phone call there's a dead body in one of my trucks, and I get here what?—an hour later? and there's no body, but you guys are all over the place. What happened, Officer?"

"Detective," Stumpf answered. "Yeah, it looks like we might need to borrow your truck here for a few days, or a while longer. What do you know about how there might come to be a body in it?"

"Nothing," Vittorio said, "I mean, I had no idea. This is a complete surprise to me."

"Were you running the store here yesterday and Friday?"

"Yeah. Gino wanted Friday and Saturday off. He usually gets Sundays and Mondays, but I didn't care, so I said, sure. Yeah, I was here."

"The whole time, both days?"

"Well, no. I had a long lunch on Friday, some friends and me. Saturday, I let my daughter, she's Alfetta, I let her open. I came in around ten–thirty."

"Did you lock up, both days?"

"Yeah, I did."

"And did you change out the USB sticks in the surveillance system, the thumb drives, before you went home both nights?"

"Uhhh,… I… I can't say I remember doing it, specifically. I usually do it. I can check…"

"No, Mr. Tonelli, that won't be necessary." Stumpf shifted in the chair, started a new line of questioning. "How many cameras do you have, and what do they cover?"

"We've got four—two inside and two outside, one in front and one in back outside."

"Do they all record to the same machine?"

"Yeah," Tonelli said.

"Were they all working, say, during the last week?"

"I know for a fact that they were when I came in on Friday," he said. "I didn't look yesterday. We can check right now, if you'd like."

"Let's," Stumpf said, and they crammed themselves into the tiny office. The monitor showed four images. "And you're sure they were working Friday morning, Saturday?"

"Positive," Tonelli said. "Friday for sure. Saturday afternoon, too. I distinctly remember checking, thinking how boring it was, nothing ever changing on those screens."

They came out of the office and Stumpf saw the team loading up their truck, their photos and fingerprinting done. "Mr. Tonelli, do you mind if we take that truck into the lab for a few more tests? We'll have it back to you by Tuesday," he said, having no idea when they would actually return it.

"That'll be okay," Tonelli said, glad that everybody was finally leaving. "Can I have your card or something, so I remember where it went?"

"Sure. Here's my card—and let's do this receipt, too. You have the VIN handy?"

They filled out the paperwork and the police left Eli, Gino, and Vittorio at the shop.

Chapter Two: Where do we start?

Detective Fred Stumpf's office would never grace the pages of *Municipal Office Beautiful*, if such a magazine even existed. Stumpf's eight–by–ten featured nothing 'beautiful,' right down to the green metal desk, piled high with scraps of paper and scribbled–on empty envelopes, to the dusty fake plant sitting crooked in its huge pot, blocking the rain-smeared single window. He came in and dropped the papers, the bag of USB sticks, and his receipt book on the desk. Then he fished the spiral notebook out of his shirt pocket and sat down.

He was pushing piles of other things across the top of his desk to make some room when Detective Jerry Redding, the other detective on the force, came in, took off his pressed sport jacket, hung it on the back of one of the two chairs and sat in the other, across the cluttered desk from Stumpf. "Now what, Tree?" he asked the stocky detective. Redding was bored with his current case and needed a piece of something interesting to recharge his brain.

Redding, fifty–eight and painfully distinguished –looking, had been the only detective in town when Stumpf got his Detective badge. Redding was, despite his affected appearance and condescending demeanor, one of the sharpest minds in policing. He paid extraordinary attention to his clothes, to the point where they called him "Mr. Blackwell" behind his back. He was a good foil, mentor, and respected partner of the disorderly but detail–oriented and dogged "Tree" Stumpf, a twenty–year veteran before he got his Detective badge last year, aged forty–three.

"We've got a dead woman in the back of a rental truck. Everything else, we don't know. We know somebody's lying, well, probably somebody's lying, or somebody's screwing around with evidence, or all of the above—or not—but we don't know who, yet. We've got three possible suspects that I've already talked to, one more that I haven't, and it's just as likely the real killer is someone we've never heard of."

"Who's the victim?"

"We don't know. And we don't know time of death, how she died, how she got into the truck, or what day, even. And if we knew all that, we'd still have nothing. She's a Jane Doe. Working on that, too."

"What's the coroner and the lab say?"

Stumpf leaned back, let out a long breath, and said, "Here, let me show you what we do have," and for half an hour they went over Stumpf's notes and hunches.

"Let's get the lab to copy these," Stumpf said, picking up the bag of USB drives. "That'll give us a week's work of something to watch."

Redding was already bored. The prospect of a few days' watching surveillance tapes didn't inspire him to volunteer to help. He picked up his jacket, brushed it with his hand and carefully put it on, straightened it, and went back to his office to work on the boring case he already had.

It was now Tuesday morning, and Stumpf called Connie. Connie Clark was sixty–something, looked fifty except for her thinning white hair, which itself wasn't a problem except that she thought it was, because in bright light she could see her pink scalp if she tried hard in a mirror. So she wore a beret. "Taupe," she called it, "because that color goes with everything." Little white curls poked out around the edges of her beret. And just like one–size–fits–all clothes that don't fit anybody, her taupe beret didn't go with anything. But she wore it except when she was alone in the station, or maybe when she went to bed, but nobody knew anything about her private life and she never talked about it.

So Fred Stumpf brought in this new case, and Jerry Redding figured he'd have a look, too. Full house.

Connie knew everything that had happened in or concerning this station since Christopher Columbus arrived during his second voyage, asking directions to Toledo. She always smiled at people who weren't on the force, and she tried to smile at Fred Stumpf, too, but she said he was just so grumpy all the time, she had to work at it.

So Stumpf called Connie. "Hi, you luscious dame," he said, using what he imagined was her preferred title. He preferred it, anyway, and Connie said it was okay with her. She got a secret kick out of watching other peoples' reactions to Stumpf's Neanderthal humor.

"The USB sticks are all copied," she said, anticipating his question. "If you'll get off my line, I'll bring the copies to you."

"Some day, I'll treat you right," he said. "I bet you'd look great in white."

"At this age," Connie said, "you mean white Spanx." She set the envelope with the USBs on Stumpf's desk.

He looked up. "Really, Connie, for all our funnin' around and all the times I'm a pain in the neck, I really do know how much you do for me––for all of us. And I truly appreciate it. I just had to say it straight out."

"What else do you need?" she said, acting coy.

"Well, now that you mention it, how about copies of all the rental records?"

She put another envelope on his desk. "You're welcome," she said. "My birthstone is tourmaline, in case you've been wondering."

"Thanks, Connie."

"Any time, Fred. Close the door?"

Stumpf nodded. Connie closed the door and disappeared down the hall.

Stumpf spread out the USB sticks, the copies, put them in order, plugged THURSDAY into his computer, pulled out a fresh sheet of paper for the case file.

The timer started at 22:11 on Wednesday night, and it showed four screens. And four cameras were working when Gino came into work at 07:48 on Thursday morning. And four cameras were working when the THURSDAY stick was replaced on Sunday morning at 07:42.

They're all working, the detective said to himself, as he went back to the beginning. He was feeling good about things. For precisely two minutes, when the time stamp on the screens got out of synch... by twenty minutes.

The indoor cameras, #1 and #2, jumped to 07:55 Thursday morning, and showed Alfetta opening the front door, turning on the computer and turning off the alarm, then walking through the shop and unlocking the back door.

The front camera showed the outdoors and was stamped two minutes earlier, as Alfetta's car pull in and she walked to the front door.

But the back lot camera, number four, was on and off all Wednesday night and into the early hours of Thursday morning. And well beyond.

Motion–activated, Stumpf surmised, irritated. *Can't cross–check timelines. Well, not easily, at least.*

Stumpf concentrated on number four and the back parking lot, including half the spot where the truck was that had the body in it. *Stamped 22:15 Wednesday, as someone walked through the lot. Too dark for color. Just shadows, no detail. Average build, pants. Didn't get close enough to the trucks to estimate height, but not an 'old' walk, so, it's somebody between, say, sixteen and maybe sixty. Hoodie—no detail on hair. Well, that really narrows it down. Didn't get near the truck, anyway.* There weren't any more records until early Thursday morning—05:55 was the first one, but it was just a time stamp; there was nothing else on the screen. *This isn't working, all right. That manager kid's right. Number four's on the fritz.*

And number four was the only one with a view of the truck. Stumpf got up. *I need coffee.* Just as he opened the door and halfway turned toward the hall, he caught a movement on the screen that snapped his gaze back to the monitor. The picture hadn't changed, but the time stamp had moved. And it was changing all the time. Stumpf sat down, took a closer look. The screen remained a fuzzy dark grey, but the time stamp was changing. The camera was detecting motion but not recording.

"Jerry, can you come in here a minute?" Stumpf shouted around the corner.

"We have telephones," he heard Connie sing from farther down the hall.

Redding came in and Stumpf turned the screen so he could see it. Redding looked at it intensely for a moment, then said, "You want to go over there, or should we just let momma bird finish raising her family?"

Stump sat, fixed on the screen, wondering if the older detective had gone off his rocker. "What the hell are you talking about?" Then, "Crap, Jerry, you're right." Stumpf sighed, defeated. "We're gonna be really lucky if anything shows up."

Redding smiled. He loved needling Stumpf. "And you're going to have to look this one over, frame by frame, too." He saw the storm clouds forming in his fellow detective's brain. "And you probably won't get anything, even then."

Stumpf surprised him, though. "Lunch?" he asked with uncharacteristic good nature.

Redding was taken aback, but he recovered. "Sure. Give me ten minutes."

Stumpf held the door for him and said, "Take all the time you need. And enjoy your lunch. I'm busy." Redding walked out and didn't look back, but he heard Stumpf's door close behind him.

Redding had figured it out in a couple seconds. A robin had built a nest in the eave where the camera was mounted. Until Wednesday, it hadn't blocked the view constantly, but that seems to have been when the eggs hatched, and momma bird started feeding her babies. As she stood on the edge of the nest, her tail feathers blocked the camera's view, and Gino thought the camera wasn't working. Vittorio looked when she was out of the nest; to him, it worked fine. Like a car's turn signal, the camera was working… not working… working… not working.

* * *

On Tuesday, Stumpf had Artie, the twenty–three–year–old lab assistant, go over the timeframe in the hope that some useful image would be in there, somewhere. While he waited, nursing his false hope, he called the Medical Examiner. "Hubert Mills, M.D."

That was the sign on the Medical Examiner's office door, and it was how Mills liked to be addressed—Doctor Mills. But in private, with the crew he had known for decades, he didn't mind being "Hugh." Once in a while. But not "Quincy," which is what everybody called him when he was out of range. Mills once spilled half a pot of coffee on Redding during a meeting when Jerry had called him "Quincy." It was twenty years ago, but the story never died.

"Hugh, what do you have on our Jane Doe, the girl in the truck?"

He raised his eyes. "Hi, Fred. I'm sending my report over, but here's the highlights. She died some time late Saturday night, maybe as late as three on Sunday morning."

"Cause?"

"This is a little unusual. She was in some kind of struggle—I wouldn't call it a 'fight.' There are grip marks on her wrists, probably from someone holding her immobile. There's a mark on her chest, looks like it was caused by her hitting her own chin there. But the cause of death is a broken neck, technically a basal skull fracture. I've sent out the x–rays to County for the forensic radiologist there to look at, but I think she broke her neck at the same time she hit her chin on her chest."

"How would that happen?"

"High speed car accident, maybe. But there's no other marks on her—no seat belt marks, no powder, abrasions, or burns from an air bag. So I don't think it happened in a car. The back of her skull isn't showing any impact damage. It's like she rolled her chin down to her chest and kept rolling. Her spine literally pulled out of her skull."

"You ever see anything like this before?"

"Fred, this is a fatal race car crash, but without a car. And it's not even a textbook car accident. I'm looking at more x–rays and a full–body MRI, checking her fingernail residue. Tox screen is out, but I'm willing to bet she's no junkie. She's given birth at least once—caesarian. No evidence of recent sexual trauma; she's not a hooker. No tattoos, either. No broken bones in her past.

There's more tests out, but that's what I've got for now."

"You're sure on the cause of death?"

"That's all I'm sure of, and the time window. I may be able to narrow that down some more, too. And it's probably not accidental. It's hard to come up with an accident that could do this to her, and do nothing else. Sorry I can't solve the case for you, Tree."

"Thanks. When you do get the case solved, be sure to call me, okay?" Male bonding.

Connie walked in with the report Fred had just received over the phone. She waited.

"Thanks, Connie." She didn't move, and Fred looked at the facial photos. The victim was in good shape for a dead person; identification might be relatively easy. "Got something else for me?"

She laid five or six papers on his desk, no envelope. Each page had the photo of a young woman on it. "Missing persons from the state, missing in the past week. Right age and coloring. Thought these might help," she said.

"They'll help. Thanks Connie. This is all?"

"It's not a popular time for young women to disappear, I guess," she said. "But look at the bright side: with only six possibles, that makes your job so much easier."

"Connie, are these just Indiana?"

"For now. I'll have Illinois, Michigan, and Ohio by the end of the day. I can get Kentucky if you want; and the whole country, for that matter. Didn't want to bury you."

"Thanks," he said, and she left.

Stumpf looked at the six Missing Persons reports. None of the photos looked like the lady in the morgue. He stood up, wanted to pace, stroke his chin in deep thought. But the office was so small and so cluttered that he had to walk out into the hall. He was pacing there when Redding bumped into him.

"Anything?" Jerry asked. Fred shook his head. "Hope you get a hit on the Missings. How far back did you go?"

"Only local so far, Jerry, and they all were reported missing in the past week."

Redding walked down the hall to Connie's desk. "Can you get Fred some more locals?" he asked. "Stay in the area, but go back a month at a time. Likelier she's local and maybe gone a while, rather than farther away and gone just a couple days."

By now, Stumpf had caught up with the older detective. "Why local?"

"She was brought *to* the truck, not brought there *in* it. Nobody likes transporting bodies long distances. Just playing the odds. I'm playing journalist here. I don't have any evidence."

Stumpf looked at Connie. "Sure," she said.

Half an hour later, Connie brought Stumpf the Missing Persons reports from roughly a hundred–mile radius, going back in time for three months. "Here's your local missing African–American women of a certain age," she said.

Stumpf stared at the first page. "Connie—does *this* woman look like," and he pulled out his photo of Jane Doe, "*this* woman to you?"

Connie squinted at both pictures. "No," she said. Stumpf was obviously surprised, and Connie continued. "She looks like her identical twin." She paused to let her words sink in, and then offered, "I'll order the dental records on this one, right away, get all the rest of what I can find out, pronto. I think you've found your girl." Connie whooshed off down the hall.

Stumpf continued looking at the reports, one from the Medical Examiner, then from Missing Persons. "Lulita Sharonda Estes," he said aloud, addressing the picture on the Missing Persons report in his left hand, then looking again at the ME's picture in his right, "I think you might not be 'missing' any more."

Chapter Three: Lulita and Daniel Estes

Lulita Estes, thirty–four, was a married mother of two girls: Sharonda, fifteen, and Lilly, two and a half. She worked in the library at Thornridge High School, where Sharonda was a sophomore. She married Daniel Estes, a thirty–six–year–old carpenter, four years ago, five years after her first husband, Sharonda's father, Clarence Nicholson, was killed in an accident at the Port of Chicago where he worked. Daniel and Lulita Estes lived with their girls in Dolton, Illinois, just within Redding's initial search radius.

"Connie, can you call Dolton and tell them we'd like Daniel Estes to come in, please? Tell him the usual: we need his help with someone who might be his Missing Person. You know the drill. Meanwhile, see what you can find out about our Lulita. Okay? I'm going back to the U–Drive–Em."

Stumpf headed for U-Drive-Em. On the ten–minute trip, he kept asking himself questions. *What's the connection? How does a young mom end up an hour away, in a truck? There's no such thing as happenstance, so what the hell happened?*

"Hello, Officer, " Gino said, coming out of the store to greet him.

"Detective," Stumpf said. "Hey, uh, Gino, right? Gino, do you have a ladder, tall enough for me to have a look at that camera out there?"

"Yeah, uh, Detective. Sorry. Yeah, we have one."

"Could you set it up for me, so I can climb up to where that number four camera is, outside? I want to talk to that kid works here, too. D'you mind?"

"No problem, Detective. Eli's here. He's in the shop. I'll get the ladder set up for you."

"Thanks. But don't go up there. Just set it up for me."

"Right. Okay."

"Hi, Eli," Stumpf said as he saw the young man, busy stacking blankets on a pallet.

"Uh, hello, sir," Eli said.

"Can we talk, son?"

"Sure—over there?" Eli motioned to the break table.

"That's great," Stumpf said. "You want a Coke or something?"

"Mountain Dew? Thanks."

They sat down. "So, Eli, how long you been working here?"

"A little over a year."

"Do you ever have anything to do with the cameras or the security system?"

"No, I... I never touch it. All that stuff's in the office. I don't have any keys to anything, and it's always locked."

"It isn't locked now." They looked and could just see it. The office door was open.

"Well, it's s'posed to be. It usually is. Anyway, I never go in there."

"Do you do any maintenance on the building, anything outside?"

"Not much. I helped with the satellite dish last summer; wind knocked it over. I carried some tar up to the roof for the guys who were patching it last April. May, maybe."

"But nothing on a regular basis? Clean drains or anything?"

"No, we have a service comes in when we need it. And we have a stick to poke into the drain holes for the regular stuff."

"When's the last time you did that?"

"Long time ago. Fall, I guess. Leaves…"

Gino came in. "The ladder's up. Do you want me to hold it for you?"

Stumpf looked at Eli. "Thanks, Eli. If I think of more questions, I'll come back, okay?"

"Sure, sir," and Eli picked up his half–empty drink and went back to the stack of blankets.

Stumpf turned to Gino. "Yeah, thanks. Let's head out there. Got a minute?"

"Let's go," Gino said.

Stumpf started up the ladder, looking out of place wearing his crumpled suit. Gino put his feet at the base of the ladder, held the rails as the detective went up, about sixteen feet, to look at the camera. The bird's nest held four tiny, scraggly–looking birdlings. Momma Bird was watching from the nearby power pole, squawking her head off.

The nest was sitting on top of the camera, tucked in just below the eave, above the camera's direct line of sight. Stumpf realized he had been looking at Momma's tail feathers which, when she'd stand on the edge of the nest, would be that blurry dark grey that triggered the motion detector, the out–of–focus dark that looked like nothing on the screen.

He started down the ladder, and Gino sneezed violently, letting go of the ladder and accidentally kicking the base. The ladder skidded about three inches on the ground, then started to slip against the building. Gino quickly regained his footing and grip, and Stumpf found out how fast he could descend a ladder. He was about four feet from the ground when Gino recovered.

"Oh, god, I'm sorry," Gino said.

"*Gesundheit,*" Stumpf mumbled, as he stepped on the ground. Gino didn't catch the sarcasm. "No harm done. Thanks. You can put the ladder away now." He headed back to the station.

Fred Stumpf's phone rang. "Stumpf… Yeah, thanks, Connie. Can you set him up in the break room, maybe give him a Coke or something? I'll be right there." He put the phone down, turned to Redding. "Daniel Estes is here. He's identified his wife's body. Victim is positively ID'd as Lulita Sharonda Estes. Husband's waiting in the break room. Enjoy your boring case. What's it about—

cigarettes?" Stumpf chuckled as he passed Redding, then got serious as he entered the break room.

"Mr. Estes? I'm Detective Stumpf. I'm so sorry for your loss. Thank you for coming all the way here. Can I get you some coffee?"

Estes wasn't what Stumpf had expected. He didn't know what he had expected the victim's husband to look like, but Daniel Estes wasn't it. A light–brown black man, thirty–six, probably six–foot five, lanky. On a guy this size, that put him at about two–ten. Jeans, white dress shirt with the cuffs rolled twice, big gold watch with diamonds, deck shoes, no socks. And a trimmed Afro. Stumpf did his best to hide his surprise. *This guy's a carpenter?*

Estes nodded to his cold Coke on the table. "I'd like to get Lulita home as soon as possible, Detective. What would you like me to do? How can I help?"

"Tell me about Lulita, her friends, her habits, anything that's new in her life. Stresses, new friends or—you have two girls, right?" Estes nodded.

"So I don't know if I should even ask if she had any hobbies, but… Especially anything new, new habits, things she did that just weren't her, you know—things that would have seemed strange a couple years ago, or a couple months ago."

"Or a couple weeks ago?" Estes asked, and Stumpf grunted in the affirmative. "Then, maybe there's something."

Stumpf looked at him, waiting.

Estes put his face in his hands, sobbed, said, "Give me a minute here," sobbed some more. Finally, he straightened up, put his hands on the table, looked at the detective. "She—Lulita—she hasn't been herself the past few weeks, maybe six weeks. She's on the phone a lot more than usual, talking to her new girlfriend, Toni. And one or two of Toni's friends. Don't know their names."

"Who's Toni?"

"I don't know. She never said. I guess she was waiting for a good time to introduce us. They did a lot of shopping together. That's new, too. She never was much of a shopper. That's fine; we don't have any money for that, anyway."

"You having money problems?" Stumpf made a point of looking directly at Estes's watch.

He was self–conscious. "Oh, this?" He held up his left arm and the TAG Heuer Carrera glistened. "Yeah, this was from a guy that I did a room addition for. I took over from some other contractor who was too slow. He was running out of time, said he didn't care what it took. He said it had to be done before his wife got home from Europe. I got it done two days early and he paid me for the whole thing. Then he said could I do him one more favor. If I would help him move all the furniture in and clean up the area outside. It was a weekend; he couldn't get anybody else to do it. So I worked my butt off for another day and a half—I didn't have anybody I could call to help out, either."

Stumpf raised both eyebrows. "Get to it, please."

"So, we got it done on Sunday night, everything. I even cleaned up the yard. I reminded him I'm a carpenter; I don't do yard work. But I was the only guy available. Anyway, I got it done. He pulled out his checkbook. I had already been paid, and Lulita, well, if I got paid more, she'd just, well, you know women… She'd just want the money. So I told him to put away the checkbook; I wanted his watch. This watch."

"And he just gave it to you?"

"Well, yeah. Pretty much. Anyway, that's how I got this watch. It's like, no matter how broke I am, I have something I can sell or pawn or something. And when I wear it, I feel rich."

"Okay, Mr. Estes. Thanks. Yeah, when you're talking about not having any money and you're wearing a watch like that…"

Estes took the watch off, handed it to Stumpf. "Look," he said, pointing to the band. "There's wear on this other hole. He had a skinny wrist."

Sure enough. "Nice," Stumpf said, "but let's get back to the important things here." He handed the watch back to Estes. "You said you're having money problems."

"No, Officer, er, Detective, I said now that it's going on to summer, we *won't* be having any money problems. There's work…" He put the watch back on, shook his wrist to wind it, out of habit.

"You *won't be,* or you *don't* have money problems? Right now, today?"

"Well, no. I mean, now that it's going on summer, I've got lots of work. But winters can be tough. Last winter, 'specially. Work was slow, and that was bad enough, but Lilly—she's our little girl—she got real sick right at Christmas, and the fridge broke down. That was, like, two thousand dollars we really didn't have."

"You late on payments? Owe people money?"

"Credit cards. I could just keep up with the minimums, barely. I'm starting to catch up now. But in the winter—you never know if you'll have work or not. It's stressful. I sneak the thermostat down…"

"What about Lulita's new friends and her shopping? When she went shopping, did she buy things, or was it just time out with the girls?"

"She bought things, I guess. I didn't pay attention, but once in a while I'd see a little piece of jewelry I hadn't noticed before. But I didn't worry about it."

"Why not?"

"Because she wasn't spending on the credit card, and I didn't see bank withdrawals, so I believed her when she said she was only playing around, spending a few dollars here and there. Apparently this Toni likes thrift stores. I didn't care if she *shopped*; I only cared if she *spent money*, and she wasn't doing that."

"Anything strange about this Toni?"

"Other than I've never met her—I assume Toni's a her—not really. It's just, she spends a lot of time…"

"Did Lulita—Mrs. Estes—have any trouble? Was she in any trouble, have any enemies you might remember? Somebody she didn't get along with? Anybody who might have caused her trouble? …Anyone with a score to settle? Anybody she owed money to?"

"Nobody. Like I said, our girls were her life. A little shopping, but she never mentioned a cross word with Toni. And not with her old friends, either."

"Do you have two cars?"

"No, just the one, and I drive it all the time… Going to my job sites. I have a guy, he brings my tools when we move to another job."

"Any idea why she would be so far from home?"

"None at all. She got lost easily, once she was away from streets she was familiar with."

She never heard of GPS? "One other thing. Could we have her cell phone for a few days? We'd like to do some analysis, look at her messages, that sort of thing."

"You need my permission? You have it."

"Thanks. But we also need her cell phone. It wasn't with… her. No purse, no ID, no shoes, no… just her clothes."

"I, uh, don't know where it is. But can't you work with her carrier? I'll give my permission, anything you need."

"It would be best to see the phone itself. The carrier doesn't have all the records we'd like to see. Maybe, you know, there's a picture of this Toni lady, or a text message that would be relevant, or something."

"Well, I'll look. I didn't think of her phone. I have a lot on my mind. But if I find it—when I find it—I'll get it to you. Her password is our address—four–five–seven–nine. But first I have to find the phone."

"Mr. Estes, Thank you again. I know this is a very difficult thing for you and your family. I hope you and your girls can find peace. In the meantime, please let me know if you think of anything else, anything that may help us catch her killer. Call any time, any time at all. And I need that phone. Please look for it as soon as you get home."

"Yes, I will. Thank you. I pray you catch her killer, and soon."

"One last thing: did you or Mrs. Estes ever rent a truck from U–Drive–Em?"

"No. Never rented a truck from anybody. Can I go now?" He started to sob and he quickly turned around and went out the door.

Stumpf turned around, left the lobby, stopped at Redding's open door. "Jerry, you ever hear of a husband, finds out his wife's been murdered, doesn't ask how she died?"

Then Stumpf went into his office, pushed aside some papers, and opened a pack of three–by–five note cards.

On each card, he wrote: Name. Description. Summary of relation with Lulita, U–Drive–Em, others in the stack. And a star rating system, one through five stars, that reminded Stumpf of his personal assessment of their believability. He gave Estes four, Eli five, Vittorio and Gino, two and three, respectively, and Alfetta, one. *And who the hell is Toni?* He made another card for Toni.

Chapter Four: Lulita's last night

Giovanni and Galena, recent émigrés from El Salvador, worked on call for a few independent contractors, when there was work that called for grunt labor and paid in cash. They had been crooks back home, escaped to Texas last February, pretended they were sick at an immigrant detention center on the border and eventually got sent to Chicago. They learned a little English. Then one day three months ago, they walked out of their official housing on Chicago's south side and relocated to Indiana. They did a spot of panhandling, stole clothes from laundromats when the customers weren't watching the dryer, and occasionally "asked" a few shopkeepers for a little money.

Galena was a strong, stubby guy with a pockmarked face that had thick black hair growing in the holes. He looked ten years older than his twenty–two years. Giovanni, same age, looked like a young Ricky Martin, except a five–foot two version. And he had a pair of front teeth that looked like Chiclets. So he looked about sixteen and let Galena do most of their talking. They had identification issued at the immigration center in Texas.

They were a team since they were kids on a dirt street on the edge of their home town, stealing from neighbors and shopkeepers, then growing into teenagers and stealing cars and the occasional propane tank or motor scooter. They even planned on taking down a bank, but somebody robbed it the day before they planned on robbing it, so they took that as a sign and gave up on robbing banks. They stole clothes and food for themselves, their siblings, and their friends. But they heard that opportunities were much better in the States, and because the locals were wise to them anyway, so they decided, not to belabor the details of the journey, to head off to "America."

They worked with Tony's "Mexicans," a couple of Cubanos named Ricardo and Ché, starting just after the snow had melted for the season. They didn't get paid much cash from them, even though they did nearly all the work, but that was okay in the short run, because they got benefits they needed, like staying in the loft and having a place to take a shower.

Once in a while, they borrowed Ricardo's rusty Olds Cutlass Ciera with two hundred thirty thousand miles on it—at least that's what it read before the speedometer broke. If he wasn't using it and they brought it back when they said they would and with a full tank, Ricardo was good with that.

Giovanni and Galena were content to keep a low profile, sleeping a lot, stealing much of their food, keeping track of regular shipments at Tony's impromptu warehouse. They saved most of the money Tony paid them.

They figured out the cigarettes right away. Ten pallets, every two weeks or so, showed up the day before they'd load them into a rental truck. The four of them could lift a pallet if they had to, but most of the time they used a Johnny Lift, a sort of hand-operated forklift that doubled as a pallet jack. The pallets would arrive on Friday, and they knew that they would be moved out Saturday night at ten.

They didn't know where the cigarettes were going, exactly. When they asked, Ché said it was none of their business, but once in a while he'd say, "Chicago." But the last time, during a nasty rainstorm, they heard the black lady driver ask if they could still unload it if it was raining like this in a place called "Doll–town." She was referring to Dolton, on the far south side of Chicago.

The cigarettes showed up on this particular Friday night. Galena asked if he could borrow the car Saturday morning if he had it back by early afternoon. The Olds was out of gas and sounding particularly wheezy. Maybe it needed a can of injector cleaner, or carburetor cleaner, or something. So Ricardo said go ahead, just bring it back full. Saturday morning, Galena and Gio went to Dolton, looking for a self–storage place that would hold ten pallets.

A ten–by–twenty, so they wouldn't have to stack anything.

Google steered them to several places. When they got within a couple miles, they took the plate off the car and threw it in the trunk. Then, they went to Storage King, and there weren't any open units, but the girl there said to try Locked & Safe, just a couple miles west.

"Hello, uh, Jilli," said Galena, reading her name tag.

"Good morning, sir How can I help you?"

"I need a space, ten by twenty. You have?"

"No, I'm sorry," Jilli said. "I'll have one on the first of *next* month, though. Could I have your name and phone number, and I'll call you? If you would like to be first on the waiting list, write down your name and your phone number and— do you have an email?" She pushed a clip board across the counter to him.

"You do no understand," Galena said. "We need today, but until Monday only. Two days. Now and tomorrow. We pay good."

Gio broke in. "We saw the empty place is four-one-nine. The first is four days more from now, Tuesday. So you do no need it now. We give you hundred dollars. We are gone on Monday, all clean and everything."

"But I…" Jilli said.

"Look, Miss Jilli," Galena said. "We only wan for today, tomorrow. We give hundred dollars. Cash, to you, not stupid Lock an' Safe place. *You…*" Gio said, Chicklets flashing against his dark features, "We nice people. You are nice person. You here alone today, Domin… Sunday, right?"

"Well, yes, but…"

"So nobody ever know. We come back tonight, you not here. We come back tomorrow night, the place is good for next customer, all clean. Nobody know, nobody fine out, and you get hundred dollars."

"But, if they find out, I will lose my job."

Galena said, "We see your car when we come in. Only one car here. Your car, right?"

A nervous Jilli looked confused, but said, "Yes?"

"You like that car?"

"Uhhh, yes," she said in a small voice.

"Then, you keep the car, get hundred dollars, we get space. We all happy. Or you say no. No hundred dollars. Something bad happen your car, maybe you. You maybe get fired, too." Galena continued, "So, you want some hundred dollars? We have a lock, too. Okay?" And he smiled.

Jilli, shaking, smiled. "Welcome to Locked & and Safe, gentlemen. Number four–one–nine. But you know that. Be sure you're gone on Monday, or I could lose my job."

"We will be all gone tomorrow night. Nice and clean. Maybe we come here 'nother time." He put the hundred–dollar bill on the counter. She took it. They drove a mile, put the plate back on, went home, filled up the Oldsmobile, parked it, and hung the key back on its nail.

* * *

Lulita arrived at Tony's, eleven o'clock, and stayed in the cab, as usual. Ché brought Galena and Giovanni around to the driver's side window and she rolled it down. He didn't look good, but he said, "Miss, Tony tell us a change tonight. Nobody there to unload, so these men go with you, okay?"

Lulita looked uncomfortable, so he said again, "Tony says this is how it is."

She sighed. "Are you ready to go?"

Galena said, "Jus' a few minute."

Back in the warehouse, Giovanni turned to Ché. "All of us, we put the Johnny Lift in the truck, too." Ché hesitated, looked at Galena and Ricardo. Ricardo was bleeding. Galena had a knife point in Ricardo's ear and was wearing an unworldly grin, dirty teeth glistening in the ghostly light. They hoisted the lift, cursing and sweating, but they got it into the truck. Then they tipped it over so it wouldn't roll around. Julita jumped but didn't look back.

As soon as the lift was stowed, Giovanni led Ricardo back into the warehouse with the tip of his blade as Galena took Ché by a painfully twisted little finger. Lulita saw the dock door go down as she looked in the rearview mirror, and knew they'd be leaving soon.

No one would find Ché and Ricardo's bodies until Monday afternoon.

Giovanni and Galena locked the side door and walked up to the running rental truck. Galena got in first, buckling up next to Lulita. Gio got in and closed the door. "You know the way," he said to Lulita, and she pulled out of the lot, headed for Dolton.

They smell bad, but I might as well make the best of this. "So, you're new with Tony?" she asked.

Gio elbowed Galena, who said, "Yes, well, no. Couple mons. We work in April, in May. For Tony, yes. You and Tony, you are friends?"

"I don't even know Tony, really," she said. "I just work for him. But you know, he pays on time. Are you from Mexico?"

Giovanni elbowed him again. "Yes, we from Mexico. You live in Chicago?" Turning it around.

"No, I live in Dolton, close to where we are bringing the cigarettes. Four–five–seven nine…" She stopped. *That's enough, Lulita!* "We'll go right past it later. We've lived there six years."

"You like it?" He was small–talking himself into her comfort zone.

"It's a nice place. Affordable, close to school."

"You go school?" he asked, a smile in his voice.

Lulita was loosening up and laughed a little. Or maybe she was so scared she couldn't think straight. "No, our daughter, Sharonda, she's a sophomore at Thornridge. That's where I work. Sophomore, that is second year in high school. Our little Lilly, she's in preschool. She's just two and a half."

Gio sort of laughed, elbowed Galena. He sort of laughed, too and elbowed Giovanni, like a couple of first-graders sitting too close together on the school bus.

Lulita suddenly felt uncomfortable, realized she had told perfect strangers about her life and family. *Get a grip on yourself, girl. They're not "strangers," really. They're co–workers. Introduced and everything. But I wish they didn't smell so bad. So open a window.*

Lulita rolled down her window a couple inches. "Is that okay with you gentlemen?" she said, as if they had a say. *At least the wind noise kills the conversation.* She started to relax. *Building trust. They'll see I'm no threat, if I'm open with them. And it doesn't smell so bad.*

As they approached Storage King, Giovanni spoke up. "Close the window, okay? It smell bad out there." Lulita complied, though she recognized the irony. "Go straight," he said, when she turned on the turn signal a couple blocks from Storage King.

"But that's where…" she started to say.

Galena pulled out his knife and said, "New plan. Go straight. We tell you where to turn. Go straight."

Gio said, "Call the truck place and say to do not worry."

Lulita called and left the message for Alfetta. Then Gio said, "Give me the phone, and stop here."

As Galena held the knife against Lulita's ribcage, Gio reset the iPhone as he walked to a puddle, then dropped her phone in it. He took the plate off the truck and carried it with him as he went back to the submerged phone, swished it around, pulled it out, and came back to the truck. "Now try it," he said. She took it, sobbing, but it wouldn't boot up. She wiped it off, shook it. It was as dead as Elvis.

Galena, sweaty face glistening in the street lights, gave directions for the next two minutes, interrupting Giovanni's instructions only when necessary.

"You not say nothing to nobody about this," Gio said. "Nobody, no matter what."

Lulita started to cry uncontrollably. "Don' worry," Gio continued. "We won' hurt you." She gathered herself up, followed Galena's directions into Locked & Safe. "You tol' us about your daughters." He wrenched her purse from under her arm and handed it to Galena, who immediately pulled out her wallet and made a point of looking at her license. He showed it to Giovanni, then carefully put the wallet back into her purse. Gently, even, and he handed her purse back to her. She snatched it, stuffed it between herself and the door. Gio continued. "Yes, we know where you live. But we won' hurt *you*." She exploded into more tears, hysterical now.

As they got out of the truck, Galena took the key. "Don' even think to open that door," he said. "Don' think at all." She collapsed behind the wheel, head down, sobbing.

The Johnny Lift was a dog to stand upright, but it did fit on the ramp. As it slid down the ramp, gathering speed, it made a racket against the ramp's corrugated surface, but it got down in one piece.

One by one, Giovanni and Galena shoved the pallets to the back of the truck and onto the Johnny Lift, then stowed them all in the space. When the last pallet went in, they left the lift under it. Gio tossed the plate inside the bed before they closed the door. Then they shoved the ramp back into place.

Galena walked up to the cab, where Lulita was in a mix of sleeping and crying. She opened the window in response to his hand signal. He handed her the key, said, "Go, and remember we tol' you." She visibly shook when he repeated her home address. "You no forget."

She shook her head, still crying, started the truck, and drove off with the window still down.

The Salvadorans walked into the dark, planning to return the following night to move the cigarettes. Maybe they did return, maybe they didn't. But they never moved the cigarettes.

Jilli locked up the office at five, so she never saw the Salvadorans and Lulita return late that night. But she made certain to check all the cameras; she wanted to know what was happening in 419. She walked past the parked car on her way out—that car had been parked for a week; a good customer was out of town, and her boss said he could leave it there. And she walked toward her apartment.

As she dodged puddles in the collapsing sidewalk on the short walk home, she kept thinking about the Salvadorans, and how she could lose her job. Just twenty–one, three years on the job, and she had done something that would get her fired.

What if Bob finds out? What can I do to cover my tracks? I can… She smiled, turned around, and went back to the office.

Jilli reset the DVR so it would over–write the earlier Saturday action with whatever happened from then on. She made a big deal out of emptying the wastebasket, something she should have done before locking up. Then she locked up and left.

Sunday morning at eight o'clock, Jilli opened the office and called her boss immediately. "Bob," she said, "did you let the customer for 419 in early?"

Bob wasn't awake. "What? Hi, Jilli. You know it's Sunday morning, right? What's up?"

"Well, I came in this morning and there's a lock on 419, not our lock, and I know we promised it to somebody for Tuesday, and I wondered if you let them in early, or what. There's no paperwork for it."

"Did you check the video?"

"Uhhh… I, um… screwed up somehow. I reset it when I left last night—I erased Saturday. It doesn't start recording until I was leaving."

"*What?*"

"I don't know what I did, Bob. Honest. I came back, after I started home, even, to empty the wastebasket. I checked the recorder and all the cameras then. I… I don't know how I did whatever I did, but… I try so hard to do a good job. I just…" And she sobbed into the phone.

Bob said, "Don't do anything with the DVR or anything. Just open the register as usual. And get out the file for 419. I'll be right over. *Don't do anything*, okay?"

"Okay. Thank you, Bob." And she let out a huge sigh of relief.

Bob arrived in fifteen minutes, unshaven and sloppy. He said, "Let's see the surveillance. What's on there?"

They watched together. Late at night they saw the U–Drive–Em, the unloading of the lift, two guys, ten pallets of... shiny something, all wrapped up. Bob watched until the truck drove off, saw Giovanni and Galena walking. "There's somebody else in that truck," he said. "Back it up." It was then that they noticed both men getting out of the truck on the passenger's side. "I'll go have a look," he said, as he grabbed the bolt cutters from under the counter. "You stay here."

Jilli watched Bob open the unit, stare inside, then close it. He didn't go in. He came into the office, said, "We have a problem," and dialed 911.

The police were there in fifteen minutes. Two officers in a squad car and a detective in an unmarked. The officers parked in front of the door to 419 and the detective came into the office and introduced himself. "Detective Martin Thurber," he said, "Dolton PD," and showed his badge. In his fifties, about six feet tall, trim, with curly blonde hair and an intelligent look about him, Thurber talked quietly and had a permanent hint of a smile on his face. Bob introduced himself and Jilli, then gave a brief rundown of what he knew.

Thurber turned to Jilli. "Is this related to the car at the end of the row, the one with four flat tires?"

She gasped. Bob looked surprised. Neither had noticed. Jilli said, "I don't know. The car has flat tires?" She looked at Bob, who shrugged. "I don't think so, but I know it didn't have flat tires yesterday when I came in at eight in the morning. I walked the whole complex."

"Did you see it this morning, or last night when you went home?"

"I… don't walk that way," she said.

"And you didn't 'walk the complex' this morning when you came in?"

"No, I didn't. I usually do, but this morning… I forgot." Bob shot her a look.

Thurber noticed. "Why did you 'forget' this morning?"

"I… I just don't know. I saw the lock on that unit, and I didn't do the walk. I called Bob right away."

Bob broke in. "Officer, I can vouch for Jilli. She has worked here for three years and has a good record. She's young, but very responsible. This morning, she did notice a lock on that unit, and she called me right away. She did the right thing." Then he turned to Jilli. "How are things between you and Jason? I know it's none of my business, but, well, you do talk about him a lot."

"We're… good, I guess," she said. "Yeah… We're good."

Thurber took over the conversation. "Let's see what happened last night. Where's your monitor?" They reviewed the night's activity. Thurber made notes. The plate was missing, but the U–Drive–Em logo was clear. Thurber made a phone call; he had heard about the body in a U–Drive–Em truck and didn't want to leave a possible lead unfollowed. Then he turned and said, "Let's go have a look at that unit." He looked at Bob. "You stay here. Let the young lady show me."

Jilli had seen the surveillance footage, but she was shocked to see everything in color. And the sheer number of cigarette cartons was impressive.

Thurber motioned her just inside the door of the unit, out of sight of the camera. He asked her, "What's really going on here? How did you make so many mistakes, all at once? "

Jilli sobbed but said nothing.

"What happened yesterday? You're not in any trouble, yet. With the law, anyway. Your boss is your problem, but I don't see any reason to bring him into this if you cooperate."

"What do you want me to say?"

"Just tell me what happened yesterday. What you tell your boss is up to you, but tell me the truth, every syllable, or you're going to jail as a conspirator in this crime."

She told him everything, even about the hundred dollars and how she reset the DVR to make sure Bob wouldn't see her taking the money "Can I keep it?" she asked, sheepishly.

"Is that the truth, the whole truth, and nothing but the truth, so help you God?" Thurber was laying it on thick, spreading out the words, *so help you God* for emphasis.

Jilli was shaking. She nodded. "Then keep it. I won't put it in my report, but..." he patted an imaginary recorder in his vest pocket, "but if I find out you're lying, or that you left anything out, *this*—he patted his pocket again—is going straight to the judge, and you're going down for a long, long time. Now, is there anything else you want to tell me?"

"No, that's everything." She hesitated. "That car—does it really have four flat tires? It didn't... yesterday morning."

"Go check on your way out," Thurber said, "and next time, do your whole job and you won't have to worry about things like that."

They came into the office. Bob had made coffee and offered some. "I've never seen so many cigarettes in my life. Jilli?" He noticed she had been crying.

"Bob, I'm so sorry. Jason... I thought it wasn't affecting me. Thanks for being so understanding. I'm sorry." Cool as the other side of the pillow.

"Well, you're still okay with me. But I do hope you two work it out, whatever it is. I need you here. You've been a good employee, and I want you here for a long, long time."

Thurber had taken his coffee to the window. He was listening to the two of them, talking behind his back but clearly within hearing range. He rolled his eyes to the sky. Then he got on his radio and called the office again, adding that they might want to call BATFE, maybe the FBI. And his cell phone rang. Stumpf said he was on the way, the truck might indeed be the one that was involved in a lot more than cigarettes; he gave a couple details, said he'd be there in a little over an hour.

Thurber went out to the officers in their car. They talked a minute, then one of them then closed the overhead door on 419 as Thurber went back into the office to wait with Bob and Jilli.

One officer stood at the door of 419, looking like a guard at Buckingham Palace, while the other left in the black–and–white. He was back in ten minutes with a couple McDonald's bags and some drinks.

The men were feasting, meals spread out on the trunk of the squad car, when a black SUV pulled up. Two men in suits approached Dolton PD officers Morgan and Reynolds. The first one flashed a badge in a little leather flip–folder at Reynolds, said, "Braintree, Bureau of Alcohol, Tobacco, Firearms, Explosives. We'll take this from here." The other agent stepped up behind Braintree, backing him up.

Reynolds looked at Morgan, and Morgan said, "We're here to secure the scene, and we're going to have to do that until the team shows up. It's his case. Once they're here, I don't care what you all do, but until they arrive," he looked at his watch and figured Stumpf would be showing up in half an hour—"in maybe another ten minutes, we're keeping this scene secured."

Braintree stepped closer to Morgan, deep into the officer's space. "We're federal officers, and we have cigarettes—that's the 'T' in 'BATFE'—under our jurisdiction. We'll take it from here."

Morgan was about to say something to Braintree, but instead looked over the agent's shoulder, and said, "Oh, crap," as another black SUV pulled up.

Braintree turned around and muttered, "Oh, great, indeed," as two more men in dark suits disembarked from their vehicle. Thurber walked out of the office, heading for all the other LEOs.

Another badge–flash from the new arrival, this time at Braintree. "Agents Black and Bleue," Tom Black said, "FBI. Looks like we're having some kind of custody battle here."

Braintree and Reynolds both nodded. Thurber introduced himself. They stood around looking at each other for an awkward three or four seconds.

Then Black said, "We were told those are Indiana cigarettes, and we're in Illinois, right? We've got this."

Each camp broke away, evidently thinking of what to do next, who would be in charge of the case, who would get the cigarettes. Who would do the smallest amount of work to get the largest amount of the loot and the credit?

These discussions went on for maybe five minutes; then Braintree said, "Screw all of you guys," and walked to the door, looking like he was going to open it.

Reynolds stepped on the handle. "Sorry. You're federal, and I'm just a lowly local cop, but I was told to secure the scene until the lead detective shows up from Indiana, and that's what I'm going to do." Morgan stood behind him, with Thurber to the side, all facing the FBI agents.

Thurber looked at the BATF agents, and said, "Now, we all know where we stand. And now we all wait."

Agent Bleue said, "And you've just put your footprint on the handle of the overhead door and probably put your fingerprints all over the rest of the evidence. I'd say you need to stay away from our case."

Reynolds said, "To avoid any more misunderstandings, let's all just back up a bit and wait for that detective. If we all want a piece of this, we're going to have to wait for him."

Everyone sullenly returned to their cars. The locals turned on their radio, reported progress so far, and when they asked when the Evidence Team was going to show up, they were told it'd be a while; it's Sunday morning. The FBI guy, Black, got into the back seat of the SUV and took a nap. Bleue paced up and down the blacktop in front of the storage units, taking note of the camera placements. The ATF agents engaged in a penny–ante game of rock–paper–scissors.

After about twenty minutes, Thurber spoke up. "Guys? If I may?" They all looked his way, happy to have something else to focus on. "The contents of this storage unit, as far as I'm concerned, are yours to fight over, once the detective in charge of the related murder case arrives and says it's okay. He won't be long; he's due right about now, er, soon, anyway. Can't we all sit tight for a couple minutes, wait 'til he gets here, and then figure out who's going to do what?"

They looked around at each other. Thurber picked it up again. "So, I'll call Detective Stumpf and find out how far away he is, and we'll all sit here for a couple minutes, maybe get to know each other better."

The Evidence Van pulled up, and there was another round of macho cop hellos. The techs were happy to get busy, pulling equipment from the van: cameras, tape measures, a little rolling measuring wheel on a stick. They started taking pictures, measuring things, and taking notes. Nobody else interfered or seemed to care.

"Hello, Detective? Yes, Detective Thurber… Uh, huh. We have our local police, BATFE, and FBI all waiting here to see you… No, no one's been inside; nothing's been touched… Okay, I will. Thank you."

With the audience waiting for an answer, Thurber said, "He's almost here." He looked toward the end of the row of storage units, where Stumpf's car was rounding the corner. "No, I lied. He's here."

"Gentlemen," Fred Stumpf said, as he stepped out of the car and adjusted his sunglasses, "Thanks for waiting. Who's who here?"

Introductions all around, then, to Thurber, "Anybody but you been in there?"

"No. Just inside this corner." He pointed to where he and Jilli had their conversation. I haven't been in there, myself. But no, nobody's been in there."

"Great." Then Stumpf asked the techs, "You mind being the Evidence Team for all of us, since nobody else's showed up?" One of them nodded consent. The other shrugged. So Stumpf swung his hand toward the door. "Well, let's open it up, get some pictures. Don't anybody go in. Agreed?"

A nod his way, and Thurber, with a vinyl glove on his right hand, opened the door.

A crapload of cigarettes—ten pallets, two by five, maybe four and a half feet high, not stacked––were along the left–hand wall of the storage unit. The Johnny Lift was in the corner near the door. Cellophane, wrapped tightly around the boxes and the pallets, held a quarter–million dollars' worth of cartons in place. After Illinois taxes, that'd be half a million. Everyone could see familiar logos, and a few more–generic–looking brands, as well. Stumpf took charge; no one wanted to be in the way of a murder investigation; everyone wanted to seize the cigarettes and go home. "Techs only, you two take all the photos of everything that you want. Get all the footprints, fingerprints, DNA, whatever—and anything else that any of us other guys wants, okay? I'm sure everybody's happy to share. Right?"

The day was getting hotter, so with knowing looks all around, the techs processed the scene. Once the scene was cleared, Stumpf took a few pictures of his own and made some notes.

Estes showed up; Stumpf had called him, asked him to drop off the kids and come over to the storage unit. Estes, as requested, had brought over the keys he had, all the keys he had found so far.

"Let's see those keys, if you will." Estes handed him the key ring. "Now, there's basically two groups of keys here, right? Is that significant, or just accidental?"

"Well, actually," Estes said, "this group here is my old key ring; this other bunch is Lulita's."

Stumpf said, "Let's go through these, one by one. You tell me what each one goes to. We'll start with yours."

"Here's my house key."

"Stop. Let's see if there's an identical key in Lulita's group." There was. "I'd like hers for evidence. Do you mind?" And Stumpf bagged the key, identifying it and taking a photo of it, laid out on the trunk lid of his car. Estes didn't notice that Stumpf's camera image included the other key rings.

They went through Daniel's key ring, matching Lulita's keys when they could, Stumpf taking hers, identifying each one, until there were only a few keys left, all Lulita's.

"And that leaves these four keys," Estes said. Stumpf reached for them. Estes hesitated. Stumpf took the carpenter's hand, gently and firmly, drew it to him, and turned it over, so that the keys dropped into another evidence bag.

"I'll write you a receipt for all these," he said. "Any guesses what they go to?"

Estes looked at them as if for the first time. "This long one looks like a Post Office box key."

"The one that says, 'USPS' and 'Do not duplicate?' What post office would you guess they belong to?"

"Yeah," Estes said, "that one. Probably Dolton, right by our house… But these other ones, they're smaller. I don't know these. More of my wife's mysteries, I guess. I hope you figure them all out, so we can catch her killer."

"Me, too, Mr. Estes. Me, too. You keep in touch, you think of anything else. And if you get any surprises, don't you go investigating them yourself. Call me before you do anything, next time, *every* time. Okay with you?"

"Sure. Listen, I'm sorry. I didn't want to bother you about something that could've been nothing. But I get it now. Sorry."

"*Nothing* is nothing, okay? Nothing that's new, nothing you find out, nothing bothers me, okay? We want to catch whoever killed your wife. We're on the same side, but we're not partners. Clear?"

"Yeah, uh… Sorry."

Stumpf's brain churned. *Sorry—for what?* "Okay, glad we're done with that. Thanks, Mr. Estes. You can go home, as far as I'm concerned, but these other fellows may want to ask you some questions."

Stumpf said a few words to the agents and local police, gave away and collected half a dozen cards, took down the names of the techs, and drove back to Indiana, leaving everyone else to sort out the cigarettes.

Redding met him as he walked in the door. "Hey, uh, Fred?" was his uncharacteristic greeting, Mr. Blackwell sounding like Barney Rubble. Stumpf stopped, receptive but confused. "Did you think that my case, you know, the boring one with all those Indiana cigarettes' showing up in Chicago, might be helped by finding a truckload of Indiana cigarettes in a storage unit in Chicago?"

"Well, yes, but not until I was already on the road. We have locals, FBI, BATFE on it, and they'll all share their information. I've got their cards. I'll make you copies of everybody's."

"Gee, thanks, Fred," said Redding, still playing Barney. Then he changed back to his regular voice, with a tiny edge on it. "Make sure I'm in the loop, okay? I need whatever you've got to help with your case, too."

"For sure, Jerry. I do have some more stuff here, including some unidentified keys…" They both walked into Stumpf's office, where Fred cleared off a small area of his desktop with his forearm. He put the evidence bags, including the one with the unidentified keys, in front of the older detective. "I've got to go log these in, but have a look while I tell Connie I'm back and get a Coke. Want one?"

"Yeah, thanks. Diet," as Redding looked into the bags.

Stumpf was back. "Here's your drink. What do you think?"

"So, did the fed boys give you any trouble?"

"Surprisingly, no," Stumpf said. "I mostly let the locals be the problem, and I acted like the guy in charge, being the murder investigator and all. There were too many of everybody for them to get organized. I mostly just went in, looked around, took a couple pictures and talked to Daniel Estes, got the keys, got their cards and their promises to share, and, well, I left."

"You're either a genius or they think you're an idiot," Redding said, "and that's a genius move, too." He smiled at Stumpf with true admiration showing in his face. "Nice job, Tree."

After Jilli locked up the office that day, she checked on the car with the four flat tires. It didn't have any flat tires. She opened her purse, looked at the hundred–dollar bill, and laughed out loud. She smiled all the way home.

Chapter Five: Crooked books

The lab finished its examination of the truck and returned it to U–Drive–Em on Wednesday. Stumpf went along and stayed after the two lab techs left in their car. Gino, Vittorio, and Alfetta were all in the office. Eli hadn't come in; he called in sick.

"Hi," Stumpf said, as he walked into the lobby from the front door and Gino was walking out to greet him. "Figured out anything yet about those USB sticks? What's the deal? You didn't know there was a bird's nest up there?"

Gino stopped. He was not expecting a question. Or at least that question. "Well, you had them three days. Did you find anything, other than the fact that we have a robin's nest?" Then he reassessed his curtness. "Sorry, uh, Detective. Want some coffee? Just made it." Stumpf nodded. "Yeah, actually. What I told you about that camera was broken, that wasn't right. I wasn't paying attention to the time stamps, didn't know we had that bird. I should have looked, but, you know, I just assumed…"

"Yeah, and you assumed wrong." Stumpf had his grump on. He led the way to the shop, to the break area, and sat down. Then he motioned for Gino to join him. "You had me thinking you might be lying to me. Glad to see you're just lazy."

Cripes, what a grouch! Gino hoped the detective didn't see how red he was turning. He held back. "I'm just busy, not lazy. I run this place, take care of everything, fix everything they leave undone, make sure everything's running right. I clean up after Alfetta's crappy paperwork. I make sure Eli gets his work done. I empty the trash, wash the floors, make the coffee…"

"What don't you do around here?"

"Well, I don't do the books or the payroll. That's Vittorio and Alfetta. But I do damn near everything else. Stopped up toilet…"

"Okay, Gino. I shouldn't have said you were lazy. Sorry for that choice of words. Sit down, calm down. I apologize, okay?"

"Sorry, Detective," Gino said, trembling. "It's just… they make me do so much, and I try to do everything their way, even when it's crazy…"

"What do you mean, 'crazy'?"

"Uh, well, like, the books. I get all the records, record all the mileage, do the maintenance or get it done—all that stuff. It would be so much easier if I just put the entries into the trucks' logs, but they do that. They're paranoid about keeping a tight hand on the books, but they don't seem to realize I give them all the information, anyway. And passing it through, I have to give explanations on some of it. It would just be so much easier…"

"But it would be more work for you, wouldn't it?"

"Yes, but less work overall. And more accurate."

"More accurate? How?"

"Well, they get the actual mileage from me. But they put it down differently, sometimes. It's always the same mileage—we don't roll back speedometers or anything like that—but they maybe put some miles on one trip, when it was from another trip. It doesn't matter, really—the total miles are always the same—but they show up on different customers."

"Any idea why?"

"Nope. Like I said, it doesn't make any sense. But, you know, it's really none of my business."

"How long has this been going on?"

"They've always kept the books."

"No; I mean, juggling the miles around. Do they do that with anything but trucks?"

"Vans, yeah. But nothing else has odometers. I mean, a car dolly…"

"Okay, dumb question. But when did you first notice they were playing games with the miles?"

"Oh, that's maybe six months ago. I found out by accident. Alfetta left some papers out, and I noticed that a truck I had just checked in—I just happened to remember the miles—that this truck's miles had been changed from the sheet I gave her. I pointed it out and she said, 'Thanks, I'll fix it,' but I checked later. She didn't."

"Any idea why she'd do something like that? Just Alfetta, or Vittorio, too?"

"Uhhh… just Alfetta. Let me think." Gino paused, closed his eyes. "Nope, just Alfetta. Like I said, it doesn't make sense. The totals always come out okay. Expenses are right; it's… well, hell, it's her business. I just work here. I shouldn't worry about it."

"Maybe not. Thanks, Gino. Anything else that's weird, anything else that doesn't make sense?"

"I still think that number four camera was broken, at least lately. I never saw an image, not for the last couple weeks, at least. And if there was motion that didn't come from that, I'm sure I would have seen something on that screen. But I would swear I didn't see anything—not even that fuzzy grey."

"Just black?"

"Yeah. Nothing. But those USBs are all recycled now. No backups. The older stuff is gone for good."

"Well, thanks, Gino. You'll let me know if you think of anything else, right?"

"Count on it, sir."

"Thanks. And, Gino, do you remember ever hearing from, or about, Mr. or Mrs. Estes?"

"The body in the truck? No, never. Nothing. You have the sheets. No 'Estes' on 'em, ever."

"We have just a few weeks of paper. Do you remember…?"

"No, and I'm pretty good at remembering customers. I don't remember anybody named Estes."

"Okay, Gino. Thanks." And Stumpf left without talking to Alfetta, Vittorio, or Eli, who decided he wasn't too sick to work today. Stumpf left through the shop, out the back way. When he went under the camera, he noticed a baby, dead on the gravel, fallen out of the nest. *And then there were three...*

Chapter Six:
Daniel Estes faces single fatherhood.

Daniel Estes thanked everyone for coming to the service. The last three days had hit him sideways, harder than anything he had ever felt in his life. His boss valued Estes and told him to take the whole week off. It was half–over, and Daniel was more tired now than when it started. "Girls, who wants ice cream?" he said, on what could be the four–minute drive home from the gravesite.

"Daddy, can we just go home?" said his step–daughter, Sharonda. Little Lilly was already asleep in her car seat. Daniel was happy to oblige.

They got home at twelve–thirty, but nobody wanted anything more to eat. It was midday, and they all went off to sleep. Even the three–year–old mutt, the one named Augie but which Daniel called "yapadoodle," was subdued. Lulita had found the little guy at the rescue. He didn't know what was going on, but he wanted to be with his "mama." And she wasn't coming home. But no one could tell him that.

Daniel turned off his phone and slept until six o'clock on Thursday morning. Sharonda and Lilly were still asleep in their rooms. Daniel noticed that he had put Lilly to bed in her fancy clothes. Then he looked down. He still had his socks on.

He went into the kitchen, made a pot of coffee, but he didn't drink coffee. But he had made coffee every morning for so many years, he just did it. *Today, I guess I start drinking coffee,* he said to himself. He took a sip. It was too hot. He set the mug on the kitchen counter, went to the bathroom, then he went back to the bedroom and got dressed *What for? I'm not going anywhere, and everybody's already paid their respects.* But he got dressed, anyway.

Back to the kitchen. *Let's try this coffee now.* He had a sip and spit it into the sink. As he poured the rest of his mug down the drain, he thought, *Gawd, that's awful. It's as awful as the last time I tried it. Acquired taste? It'll take another two or three lifetimes for me to acquire that taste.*

He spit, rinsed his mouth, spit again. Then he turned and grabbed the coffee pot, turned off the coffee maker, and dumped the rest of the coffee. *Sorry, Luli, maybe in the next life, but not in this one.*

Sharonda wandered into the kitchen. "I can't believe I slept so long," she said. She reached into the pantry for some Cheerios, went to the fridge, opened it, looked around... and closed it. "No milk," she said. She opened the freezer and found half a box of Eggos, put them all in the big toaster, and pushed the handle down. Then she went back to the pantry and put the Cheerios away, looked around for some syrup. "No syrup," she said as the Eggos popped up. She opened the fridge again and got some margarine, smeared some on the plate, put the Eggos on top, and put the margarine away.

All this time, her stepdad was watching. "Thanks," he said, "I'd love to share." But Sharonda pretended not to hear him, kept her back to him, and walked her plate out to the table by the television in the living room.

"Sharonda, you know we don't eat there," he said.

Without saying a word, she picked up her plate and fork and walked into her bedroom, shut the door. Daniel was too drained to say or do anything.

Lilly was crying, something about how she was stuck in her covers. He went into her room and unwrapped the 30–month–old, who had sweated about a half–gallon of water overnight. *Poor kid. She's soaked.* And sweat wasn't the only thing she was soaked in.

Daniel took Lilly into the bathroom, sat her in the tub, and gave her a squirty–bath, their ritual play–way of getting Lilly wet all over. Daniel got the water temperature just right, then unhooked the shower head, and pretended to chase an imaginary spider all over Lilly, until they were both wet and exhausted, and Lilly was clean. He dried her off and told her to run into her room and put on her jammies

"Jammies are for sleepy, Daddy," she said.

He picked out some clothes, helped her dress, and walked her out to the kitchen, hand in trusting, tottering little hand. A sticky plate and fork were lying in the sink.

"Sharonda, come in here and rinse your dishes," he shouted half–heartedly, "and empty the dishwasher." No answer; he heard the shower running. He rinsed the plate and fork, emptied the dishwasher, and put Sharonda's breakfast things in it.

Daniel sat down and pulled Lilly up on his knee. "Does Lilly–boo want breakfast?" he said to the smiling little girl, not thinking what he was going to make for her when she said she did.

"Breakfast, Daddy," she said, half–hopping up and down, but still sitting, clapping and smiling. She dropped herself to the kitchen floor, sat there in anticipation.

"Okay, Lilly–boo, here comes breakfast! Daddy's going to make you breakfast!" *Out of what?* He rummaged around in the pantry, spied some spaghetti and an unopened jar of clam sauce. "Daddy's gonna make Lilly–boo a white sketti breakfast," sounding as enthusiastic as he could. Lilly didn't seem to mind. She didn't know what white sketti was, but then neither did Daniel until half a minute ago.

He was boiling the pasta, three minutes 'til done, when Sharonda walked in and saw the clam sauce that he was putting into a dish to microwave. "Oh, my god, Daddy," she said. "You're making *that*? Eewww." And Lilly started to cry. *White sketti isn't going to work. Thanks, Sharonda.*

Daniel was desperate, but he didn't want to let his frustration add tension to the relationship he already had with Sharonda. "Don't help any more for now, okay," he said to her, edge on his voice, but controlled, not loud. "Just get ready for school."

"I'm not going to school today," she said. "I have the week off, remember? Mom died."

Daniel bit his tongue but shot back, his tone civil, masking a growing rage inside, "Then go to your room. And stay there, until I tell you to come out." She started to huff past him, but he grabbed her arm and stopped her. "And give me your phone."

She slapped it into his hand, walked away. Her door closed, shook the hallway.

Daniel looked at Lilly, who was finishing up her crying, unsure why she had started. He looked in the fridge. *Saved!* "Lilly–boo, no white sketti today. Today, Daddy's making *red* sketti." She clapped and he squirted the ketchup on two bowls of spaghetti. He sat on the floor and they ate red sketti together. Lilly didn't see how wet his eyes were.

Sharonda came out of her room as Lilly and her dad were finishing breakfast, looking contrite.

"I'm sorry, Dad," she said. "I'm… we… I guess it's going to be hard for a while. I am sorry. I love you." She rested her head on his chest, he put his hand softly on her back. Then she said, "Can I have my phone back, please?"

Daniel was wary to begin with, so he wasn't angered by Sharonda's transparent ploy. Instead, he said, "I love you, too, Kiddle. We're just going to have to be kinder to each other, more patient. Lilly needs you to look after her today, while I go through some of Mom's things—paperwork, accounts, all that legal stuff."

"Can I have my phone back? Please?"

"Yes, of course." She smiled and held out her hand. He didn't smile. "Tomorrow, if you're nice to Lilly all day."

So Daniel Estes went up to the master bedroom, their bedroom, now just his bedroom, and sat on the bed for a moment, wondering where to start. *Anywhere is better than nowhere. Her drawer.* Lulita had one drawer in the top right of the old fashioned dresser, that was exclusively hers and as private as her purse. Daniel had his own drawer in the nightstand, the bottom one, that Lulita never saw him open. It had a little lock on it, and she never knew, never asked where he kept the key.

So Daniel opened Lulita's drawer, took a deep breath, pulled it the rest of the way out, and dumped it on the bed.

Which was a mistake. Dirt, sand, little stubby eyebrow pencils, regular pencils and some shavings, a leaky but dried–up ballpoint pen, shirt pins, stray staples, and an old bottle of ink with the rubber bulb cracked—all that was in the drawer, now on the bed. *Idiot.*

Well, let's see what else there is. Daniel found a little notebook with the passwords for her computer accounts and software, Office, eBay, their bank account. She handled that stuff, and the computer always stored the password, so if he wanted to see something, it popped right up. He put the notebook aside. *That's important.*

Elastic hair thingies, an old key to a safe deposit box, a cheap plastic pencil sharpener, coupons that expired two years ago, a card with Lilly's doctor's phone number, and her next appointment, scheduled in two weeks. Plus a little bottle of perfume, a novelty pocket knife that had all the Swiss Army stuff on it, in Minnie Mouse size… magazine renewal slips, and some of the costume jewelry that Lulita was so fond of. *She only got the good–looking stuff. Doesn't look cheap. But she liked it, so what the heck?* And a plastic tube with… gold coins. *Twenty gold coins? Twenty ounces of gold?*

Daniel knocked on Sharonda's door. She turned around and he said, "I'll need you to watch Lilly for a little while. I've got some things I have to do downtown."

"Downtown? Chicago? Can I come?"

"No, honey. Just Dolton. Shouldn't be long. I'll call you if it's going to take more than an hour."

Sharonda turned back to her computer and Daniel went to their bank. "I'd like to remove my wife's name from our account," he told the teller. She motioned him to a room off to the side of the lobby and said, "I'll have the Vice President meet you in a moment. I'll get everything ready. In the meantime, the coffee's fresh. Help yourself." She whirled around and headed out of sight around the corner.

In a moment, a tall brunette with long hair, blue silk blouse, and a short tight brown skirt that looked like it was made out of the seat cover from an old pickup truck, approached Estes, and extended her hand, even as he rose to greet her. "Hi, I'm Julie Franks," the VP said. "I understand you want to take your wife's name off your joint accounts. Do you mind telling me why?"

She's the VP? I've got to get her number. He was feeling momentarily dizzy. *Cripes, Daniel! You should be ashamed of yourself! Focus, man.* "She was murdered this weekend." *Accounts? Plural? Maybe she has a lisp.*

"Oh, oh, I'm so sorry, Mr. Estes. I read about that. Horrible. I'm so sorry. Sure. I see you brought your statement. I know your story, but I do need to see some ID."

Did she look interested? I've got to come back in a few months... He snapped out of it and signed the papers that she gently pushed to him across the table. Then she gave him another stack of papers. "Do you want to take her name off the other account, too?"

"Other account?"

"Yes, the one you two opened just after Christmas. The college fund."

Daniel recovered on the outside. "Oh, sure. That'd be fine." *Another account? I thought she told me these were to get updated signatures on the account. Some new banking rule, went into effect January first.* "I didn't know we had to open a new account, just for that. New rule?"

"Well, Julie said, "we get new rules all the time, but that's not it; this is a different account."

"Can we just close it and put the funds into the old account? I mean, if there aren't any rules about that."

"Sure. You're on both accounts. I'll get the papers to close the account. Then you'll make a deposit to the account you're keeping."

"How much was in the account, if you don't mind my asking?"

"Uhhh, let's see. Ninety–six thousand, two hundred and six dollars, even. I'll be right back." And she left.

Estes didn't want to shake, but he couldn't control his left hand. He put it under the table, grabbed his knee and held on, hard. *Ninety–six thousand dollars?* He had no answer.

Julie came back with half a dozen papers to sign. Then she said, "I see your wife had a safe deposit box. Would you like to go see what's in it?"

"I brought the key," he said, and Julie Franks led the way to Lulita's box. Estes was getting squirrelly inside, hoping the key he found in her private junk drawer was the one he needed. He felt sweat on his fingertips as he rubbed the key between his thumb and forefinger. *Damn, I'm glad she knows what box it is.* She put her key in the box; he put the key in the other lock and it turned. Julie Franks left the room. Daniel Estes opened the door, slid out the box...

He left the childrens' birth certificates, his and Lulita's marriage certificate, papers about his bankruptcy five years ago, but he took three short tubes of gold coins, ten coins in each, and he left the bank, walking slowly, dragging, like an old man. *Ninety–six thousand, two hundred and six dollars? Thirty more gold coins? Plus the gold at home—that's, like, another seventy thousand altogether.* He felt the plastic tubes, heavy in his pocket. *Maybe a hundred and seventy thousand dollars, that she never said a word about. God, Luli! What were you planning? What were you*

doing? When did you get it? He was trembling.
Am I going to get in trouble? Of course it's trouble!
Good God, Lulita! What am I going to tell the
cops? Then, with a whole new level of terror
gripping him, *What has the bank told the IRS?*
Estes walked right past his parked car. Three cars
down, he stopped, turned around, and stood there
on the sidewalk for a few seconds. *What the hell*
am I supposed to do? I've got to tell that detective
something. But how much should I tell him? How
much does he already know? Oh, man, I'm screwed.
Rich but screwed: didn't think that was possible. He
laughed at himself, drove home.

He waited for the garage door to close, walked
into his house, and sat down at the kitchen table.
Sharonda was on him in a minute. "Okay, Daddy,
my phone. Please." He handed it to her without a
word, and she left without a word. His mind was
ablaze, his thoughts dancing like flames, no
pattern.

He called Stumpf. "Hello, Detective. Dan Estes,
Lulita's husband? I've got some unexpected news.
Don't know if it relates to the case, but…" Estes
decided to tell him about the ninety–six thousand,
two hundred and six dollars, and neglect to
mention the gold coins. "…so what do you want
me to do?"

Stumpf, by this time, was sitting down at his
desk, cell phone on speaker so he could take

notes. His little spiral book was in his suitcoat pocket hanging limp near the door, so he grabbed a yellow legal pad, brushed a few pages of something else over the top binding, and started on a fresh page.

Redding was walking past his door and Stumpf waved him in and pointed to the phone. The senior detective picked up the pile of papers that was on the nearest chair, set the mess on the floor, and sat down.

He punched the speaker button. "So, Mr. Estes, what do you have for me?" Stumpf said.

Estes told him of Lulita's secret account and the ninety–six grand, and repeated, "What do you want me to do?"

"Where is the money now?"

"I put it into our original joint account and closed the one I didn't know about. It's all still in the bank."

Redding looked at Stumpf, rolled his eyes.

Stumpf said, "So you've commingled the accounts, is that it?"

"Is that it?" a confused Estes replied. "I guess so." Then, "So, hey, is that my money now, or what?"

Stumpf looked at Redding, then said, "We—you—don't even know if that was your *wife's* money, right? You'd best not spend it, and we all had better find out how it got there. If it's hers, er, if it was hers, and it's in your joint account, well, then it's yours. But that isn't my call, and certainly not until we figure out where it came from. You didn't have any idea your wife had ninety–six thousand dollars in a new account?"

"No, none at all. Like I told you, I didn't realize we even had two accounts."

"You have the bank statements from that account, all of them?"

"I'll get them to you tomorrow. Do you need certified copies, or can I just ask the teller for them and scan them?"

"For now, just scan them and get them to us. And I want you to think, real hard, about where that money came from and why you didn't know about it. I'll be here by nine your time, and I'll be expecting to see those statements and hear your ideas before my second cup of coffee. My email is on my card."

"Yeah, uh, okay, Officer uh, Stumpf. Will do."

"Detective Stumpf. I'll be waiting. Think, Mr. Estes, where could an extra ninety–six thousand dollars come from? Think, or you're gonna force us to guess."

Well, that was rude! I did this for him! Grouch. "Right. Detective. Sorry. Yeah, I wanna know, too. Thanks."

Daniel Estes hung up, walked to the fridge, got out two ice cubes and put them in a glass. He walked to the liquor cabinet and appraised its contents, shook his head and then went to the faucet and poured water over the ice. He sat down and pulled a tube of gold coins out of his pocket. He hefted the heavy tube, feeling its weight, its warmth. He wasn't thinking about its valuation; this was something more like comfort.

He poured the coins onto the table in front of him and admired their perfect shine. Then he started to put the gold back into the tube and stopped. He poured out the coins again. *I've got fifty ounces of gold, like three pounds of gold, that nobody knows about.* He thought a moment. *Probably not any worse than having one ounce that I didn't tell that detective about. 'It's the principle of the thing,' right?*

He put the coins back into the tube, put the tube in his pocket, and walked over to the fireplace. *I can always tell him I found them later.*

He gazed at a small framed picture of Lulita, sitting on the mantel, taken when they had just met. She looked as young as Sharonda, but she was maybe twenty in the photo. In pigtails, and she never wore pigtails except that one day. A tee-shirt, jean shorts with suspenders built in. They didn't show, but he remembered she had on some awful old dirty white sneakers and no socks.

He hung there for a moment, husky forearms resting on the mantel, eyes just a couple inches from the picture glass. *Baby, what were you doing? Why didn't you tell me? When were you going to tell me? You were going to tell me, weren't you? What were you doing with all this money, and how did you get it all, and so fast?*

He paused for a moment. *And whose is it, really?*

Estes dumped the ice water in the sink and went to bed. He was awake most of the night, up and shaving by seven, making breakfast at seven–thirty.

Chapter Seven: Alfetta and Tony

Two days before Daniel opened the safe deposit box, Alfetta fished her phone out of her purse, tried to speed dial, sighed, canceled the call before it connected, and sat down. *You're losing it, girl.* She unzipped the little pocket in her purse, pulled out the beat-up old iPhone, turned it on, and waited until it lit up.

"Hi, Tony? It's me. Did you hear about Lulita? …She did?... But where's… But that's impossible! That was our whole thing! We have to talk… No, in person… The usual place. Can you get there in… Okay, I'll see you at seven–thirty." She turned off the iPhone, zipped it back into her purse.

Tony Gemelli rolled up to the Cracker Barrel in his dark–blue Mercedes and saw that Alfetta's silver Miata was already there. He parked on the other side of the building.

"Hi, Tony," she said, looking small, sitting on the bench by the door and holding one of those vibrator–light things that they give you when you have to wait for a table. "I just got here."

The dining area was full, but they were the only ones waiting. He sat next to her. "Nobody else here out front. So let's talk while we can. Poor Lulita. Sad. So, where's the product?"

"Jeezuz, Tony, I just found out yesterday afternoon. She's my friend. Give me a minute."

"You're her partner. That means everything she does, you do. Everything she's responsible for, you're responsible for."

"She just got the place, big enough for everything. And I've got the trucks. Everything went fine on the early runs. You got your cigarettes, didn't you?"

"Those were test runs. You knew that. Six months, I let you build up your operation, build my trust. Well, I don't trust either one of you any more, and I don't have my cigarettes."

"Lulita's dead, Tony."

"Then I don't trust you twice as much. I'm on a schedule here. Those need to get delivered tomorrow." His face and tone softened. "Look, just tell me where they are, and I'll send another crew. You won't have to bring them to the cottage." He wasn't going to say "Storage King."

"Tony, I don't know where they are. Lulita called me from the storage place she was supposed to go to, said your guys told her she had to go to a different place and she'd call me with all the details when they got unloaded. But she never called me. I don't know what happened."

"'My guys' never told her anything. I told her where to deliver, same as always. She picked up the cigarettes, right?"

Alfetta felt something very much like claws digging into her back. She swallowed. "I—I assume so. I mean, she told me she was going to be unloading. She wouldn't be unloading an empty truck, would she?"

"You tell me. You're the truck lady."

"The mileage was right. In fact, it was about eleven miles too far. That could easily be odometer error." *Why did I tell him that? Alfetta, you're a moron.*

"It could just as easily be driver error," Tony said. "A little side trip."

"To where?" Alfetta was frantic on the inside.

"To where, precisely," Tony said, as the vibrator/light thingie vibrated and lit up. "Table's ready," he said. Then with a grand gesture, "Shall we?"

Menus, water, no drinks, just water, thank you. Yes, we'll need a few minutes… Lots of people; lots of noise. Old couple nearest them were shouting at each other, just to be heard.

Tony said in a low but gentle–sounding tone, "So Lulita was in your truck? How do you figure that happened?"

"I don't figure anything, Tony," Alfetta said. "That wasn't even the truck she used."

"What?"

"That truck was in the lot from Thursday on. She must have used a different truck, not one of mine. That's my story, in case I'm asked."

"Where's the one she used?" Tony wasn't usually this dense.

Alfetta rolled her eyes. "Of *course* it's the same truck, but according to our records, it never left the lot. Neither did the van and those trucks the other times." She let go an exasperated sigh. "It went out Friday night with Lulita and was back before dawn on Saturday. I fixed the records. It never left."

"Don't you have cameras in that Podunk town? At least, in your lot?"

"The one that matters doesn't work."

"So how did your partner wind up in a different truck?"

Alfetta leaned forward. "Damned if I know. Same truck, different truck… Truck didn't go out that night."

Tony was confused again for a moment; then he got it. He leaned over the table, said in a low voice, "And, to the point, where's my damn cigarettes?"

Just as quietly, as if they were having an intimate conversation, Alfetta leaned forward and whispered, "Tony, there's a good chance they're just gone."

He was straining to keep his voice pleasant and on the quiet side. Veins bulged on his forehead, his neck. "Look. If they're gone, you owe me two–fifty large. Tomorrow. Then interest, twenty percent."

"Twenty percent?"

"A day."

Astonished, looking maybe like she was having fun. "That's impossible!"

"Keep your voice down… So find my cigarettes. I won't be offended if you leave before your meal gets here."

Calm again, more like his mother: "Tony, we haven't ordered."

"Finish your water, then go."

Alfetta left. She didn't need water. She needed time.

Chapter Eight: Death begins at forty.

Stumpf's phone rang. It was Gino.

"Detective Stumpf? I think something doesn't add up. You said to call if I noticed something strange."

Stumpf fumbled for his little notebook. "Yes, Gino. What's strange?"

"Well, remember I told you that sometimes I thought the mileage was messed with? I have an example for you."

"Tell me, Gino. Slow and easy. I'm listening."

"Well, I just got that truck back from your lab, you know. The one with, with the lady in it. I remember it had almost exactly forty thousand miles on it when it came in last week. It was, like forty–oh–oh–six, I mean, just over forty."

"What about it?"

"Well, did your lab guys drive it around a lot?"

"How much is 'a lot?'"

"Like, two hundred and thirty miles? Two–forty, maybe."

Stumpf hesitated, then said, "No way. We took it to the lab and back. No side trips. Twenty, twenty–five miles, tops. I'll check, but that'd be a maximum. You think it went another two hundred? When?"

"That's what's confusing, Detective. According to our records, that truck didn't go out at all. But it has two hundred and something extra miles on it."

"I agree. Confusing. Can you check the records on that truck?"

"I did," Gino answered. "The mileage is okay in the records, back to the first of the year, at least. It's just that, well, I remember the mileage. I remember thinking it must have been cool to watch the odometer change to forty thousand, and I was sorry I missed it, and now..."

"Now it's—what's the exact mileage on it now, Gino?"

"Exactly forty thousand, two hundred and thirty–one. Point six."

"So..."

"So," said Gino, "So somebody took that truck and drove it a couple hundred miles and then made it look like it didn't go anywhere. Buried the mileage back a few months."

"If your memory's right."

"Yeah, of course. But I *remember*..."

"Okay, Gino. Thanks." Stumpf thought a minute. "Gino, do you have any other twenty–footers that recently turned forty thousand?"

"Uhhhh, Yes, but not that close. We have one that's forty–one thousand and something. But that one turned forty, two weeks ago."

"Did you check the records on that one?"

"Uhhh, no. No, I didn't."

"Would you mind having a look, see when that one turned forty? Where it's been, who rented it, when it went out and came back, all that? Start

with the last time it was under forty thousand.
Then get back to me."

"Will do, Detective." They hung up.

Chapter Nine: Alfetta's math

Alfetta was still hungry. She picked up a double cheeseburger at the drive–through on her way back to the U–Drive–Em, and it was still stuck halfway down her gizzard when she got there. She made a beeline to the drink machine, where the only thing left was Mountain Dew. *Better to die of this than choke to death. Probably.*

Gino was surprised to see her. "What's up, Alfetta? Everything okay?"

She didn't answer, though. Avoiding the question, she looked away and said, "I'm busy." She went into the office and closed the door. She flipped on the screen and pulled up the records of the truck. *Dammit. I can't get back to the actual mileages. All these records are so messed up. By me, even. Fine job of faking the history. Now I can't even do my own detective work.* She opened the door. "Gino, you there? Can you come in here a minute, please?"

Gino came in and she motioned him to look at the screen, over her shoulder. "Gino, I think something's wrong with these records," she said. "Like this damn truck, the one that just got back from the police. I could have sworn it didn't have forty thousand miles on it just a week ago. How many miles did they drive it, anyway?"

"Uhhh, yeah," he said. "I wondered that, myself. I thought I remembered that it was just over forty thousand, just a couple miles, when it came back from that last rental. But then, I mean, now it's got a lot more on it."

"You have any idea how?"

"No, not really. I mentioned it to the detective, but we checked the records back, for months, and I finally just thought I was losing my mind."

"Do you think the police drove it somewhere?"

"I even asked the detective. He said maybe twenty miles. I think he finally said it should have been, like, twenty–two and a half miles, that's all."

Alfetta took a deep breath. "So, you already talked with that detective and told him you thought the miles were wrong, but you couldn't prove you remembered it right? He said they put on just twenty–two miles?"

"Yeah, and a half. Can I get back out there? I've got a customer waiting."

"Sure, Gino. You should have said something. Get out there. Thanks."

Alfetta was doing math in her head. *Forty thousand, two hundred thirty–one, point six minus twenty–two and a half, and the distance from here to where she was supposed to be going was…*

Think, Alfetta! Ninety–nine miles. So that means, she went about five miles out of her way, maybe less, depending on how much over forty thousand it really was, if she bought gas, whatever… So she diverted no more than two and a half miles from where she was supposed to go. Probably less, turning around, going through rows of storage units, all that. She pulled up InterMaps.com and anchored her search at the planned destination, drew a circle around it with a two-and-a-half mile radius. *It's in there!*

There were only two other storage units in the circle. She wrote down both phone numbers and called the first one. "Hello, Keep–Ur–Key. This is Julie speaking. How can I help you?"

"Hi, Julie. This is Kate," she said. "Listen, do you rent ten–by twenties? Do you have any available? And how much?"

"Gee, Kate, I'm sorry. Our biggest is an eight–by–ten, and anyway, it looks like we don't have any coming open for one of those until, uhhh, September at the earliest. Would you like me to take your phone number and email, and let you know if one becomes available earlier?"

"No, thanks, Julie," Alfetta said. "Say, do you know anyplace else nearby that has big units?"

"Well, there's Locked & and Safe, but I don't know if they have any that big. And Storage King. I know they do, but of course I don't know what they have open."

"Thank you, Julie. You're a big help. I'll call them."

Storage King! Okay, mapping software, how far from Storage King to Locked & Safe? Aha—two miles!

"Hello, Locked & and Safe? This is Kate, uh, Townsend, and I'm moving into the area next week, looking for a ten by twenty storage locker for a few months. Do you have anything available?"

"Sure, Kate, did you say? Hi. I'm Jilli. We just rented out our last one, but… let me check on something. Hold on just a second."

Alfetta listened to elevator music. *Sounds like Devo plays Mozart's lesser–known bombs.* "Kate? Are you still there?"

"Yes. Do you have something?"

"It looks like we may have that one I told you about—coming open again in a couple days. Would you like to reserve it?"

"When, exactly?" Alfetta asked. "I need to rent a truck and I don't want to be sitting around running up charges."

"I, uh, can't give you an exact date," Jilli said. "It's a little unusual."

"I can keep a secret, girlfriend. What's up?"

"Well, Sunday, a whole bunch of police came here and, well, the unit was all full of cigarettes. Right now, they have it all locked up, but they're coming back as soon as they know what to do with them. The guy that was going to get the unit said he couldn't take it late and he was going somewhere else. So when they're gone, like, a couple days maybe, you can have the unit. Okay?"

"Kate" hung up.

Alfetta closed the screen windows that were open, erased the last hour of her browsing history, and slumped back into the chair. She dug the scratched and cracked iPhone out of her purse. "Tony? Hi, Alfetta… Just shut up a minute, Tony. I found out what happened. It's good news and bad news."

"Give me the good news," he said.

"Well, actually, it's all bad news. I found the cigarettes."

"That's good news."

"No, not really. The police found them first. And they were at a different storage yard, not Storage King. Two miles from there."

"That's not good news. So, well, how'd they get there? You and your BFF planning on keeping them hid?"

"Tony, I didn't know where they were! And Lulita—she didn't have any way to unload them. Your guys did that. *Your* guys—they hijacked your cigarettes and my truck. *It's your guys did it!*"

"So, the police tell you this?"

"Well, no. I figured it out."

"How? How do you know where the cigarettes went? That my guys hijacked the truck? That the cops already found them? How?"

"Well, I started thinking…" and she told him the whole story.

Tony didn't say anything. He was at home, alone, in his South Loop apartment, about to have a drink and plan… something. "Alfetta, you and your partner still owe me two hundred forty–eight thousand, three hundred and ninety–one dollars and sixty cents, which you need to pay me by when interest starts accruing."

"Tony you know that's impossible. I…"

"But I think you may be able to work off a big part of it. You follow me?"

"Not at all, Tony, but… what choice are you giving me?"

"It's not a choice, exactly. Think of it as an opportunity."

"What do I have to do?"

Chapter Ten: Ferguson and Plessy

Alfetta called Stumpf. "Hi, uh, Detective Stumpf? Alfetta Tonelli, from U–Drive–Em. I, uh, think I might have come across something that could help the case."

"Should I come over? You have something to show me? Or can you tell me?"

"Both. Uh, either. But I, uh, want to talk to you in private."

"Come to the station. I'll be there in two minutes."

"Okay."

Connie Clark hadn't seen Alfetta before, so she stopped her at the door. "Hello, miss. Are you here on business? Can I help you?"

"I'm Alfetta Tonelli, here to see…"

And Stumpf walked up to her. "Glad you're here, Alfetta." He turned to Connie. "This is the lady who owns the truck that our Lulita was found in."

"I see. Nice to meet you." Connie nodded, went back to work.

Stumpf led Alfetta to his office, took a big pile of papers from the corner of his desk nearest the door and put them on the floor next to the dusty fake plant's pot near the window. Then he picked the papers off one chair and put them on the stack that was forming on the other one. "Please, Miss Tonelli, have a seat." Alfetta sat, balanced on the edge of the chair. He went to his own chair and picked up the papers in the middle of it and stacked them atop another pile. "What's on your mind?"

"I can get you the guy who I think killed my friend."

Stumpf just looked at her.

"But I need help and a deal."

Stumpf kept looking at her, waiting. His chair was more comfortable than hers, and they both knew it.

"I need a deal," she repeated.

"How big a deal?"

"I don't want to go to jail."

"Did you kill Lulita Estes?"

"No."

"Do you know who did?"

"Not exactly, no."

"Then I can't exactly promise you a deal, can I?"

She threw her hands in the air. "Okay. What do you want me to say?"

"Just tell me what you know. That's a start. Close the door."

She didn't have to get out of her chair. She just reached, grabbed the edge of the door, pushed it shut. Stumpf centered a fresh yellow pad on his desk in front of him. He brought a pen out of his drawer, put his arms down on the desk, leaned forward, and looked at her. "And what happened?"

"It's about cigarettes," she said.

"They're bad for you. I already know that,"
Stumpf said. "What else you got?"

"It's about a whole lot of cigarettes. They were
stolen."

"You stole cigarettes?"

"No—they were stolen from me."

"You're reporting a robbery?" Stumpf was
playing with her. "How many cigarettes?"

She didn't like that. "Stop it, please. I'm in big
trouble, and I can help your case if you help me.
How about ten palletloads of cigarettes, bought in
Indiana and brought to Illinois to be distributed?
Now are you interested in helping me?"

"So somebody stole your cigarettes, a whole lot
of cigarettes, that you were planning on selling in
Chicago, and what?—You want me to help you
get them back?"

"No. I don't sell cigarettes. I just get the trucks.
Lulita drives. But she was robbed, hijacked.
Lulita's my friend, and she's dead."

Stumpf hadn't written anything on his yellow
pad. He showed her the blank page, then said,
"Alfetta, I don't do cigarette cases at this time. We
have another detective here. He's here right now,
in fact. I just saw him. He's knee–deep in
cigarettes. Could you tell him your story?"

"No, I want to talk to you. This is about Lulita,
too. But still, I need a deal."

"Do you have a lawyer? Because I think you're going to want to have one. Maybe tell your lawyer first." He walked around the desk, stood between her and the door. "Alfetta Tonelli, I'm placing you under arrest for conspiracy to evade taxes and as an accessory in the murder of Lulita Sharonda Estes, and for transportation of bootleg cigarettes across state lines, with intent to sell." He was making most of these charges up, didn't know the names of the formal charges, but they had the effect he wanted. He continued. "You have the right to remain silent..."

When he finished with reciting the Miranda speech, she looked up at him from her chair, and said, "I'd like an attorney, please."

"Stay there," he said, and he stepped out of his office and called down the hall.

"Connie, can you please get our Miss Tonelli a lawyer? And can you find Jerry for me, please?" He went back into his office. Alfetta hadn't moved.

Redding showed up a minute later. No room to sit, so he closed the door behind him and leaned back against it. "What's up, Detective?"

Stumpf said, "Detective Redding, Miss Alfetta Tonelli here has a truck that was used in the transportation of a lot of cigarettes between somewhere in Indiana and somewhere else in Illinois, near Chicago. Oh—and that same truck seems to be the one in which Lulita Estes was found in a plastic bag... In. I told her you were on the cigarette case."

Redding looked at Alfetta, looking small and pathetic in the chair. But he spoke to Stumpf. "What does she know about cigarettes?"

"Nothing, 'til she gets a deal."

But Alfetta spoke. "I know that ten pallets of cigarettes from Indiana were found Sunday in a ten by twenty foot locker at Locked & and Safe in Dolton, Illinois." And she clasped her hands together and thumped them onto the desk, making a big deal of it. "No more until I get a deal."

Redding looked at Stumpf. "She tell you this?" Stumpf shook his head. "You tell her?" Again, no. "Then how does she know?"

And Alfetta took the bait. "I made a few phone calls, used the Internet. Asked some questions, did some math. I figured it out. But there's more, a lot more, and I'm waiting for my lawyer." She looked at Stumpf. "You're getting me one, right?" And he nodded.

"You make your phone call yet?" Stumpf asked. She shook her head, started to dig in her purse. "No, Miss Tonelli, you use our phone. Here. Do you know the number?" She nodded again.

When the other end picked up, she said, "Daddy? Daddy, I'm down at the police station. I'm under arrest. They're getting a lawyer for me… No, I'm okay, really… Thanks, Daddy." She handed the phone back to Stumpf.

Everyone stayed in place, silent, as though they were all thinking up their next moves.
Redding wanted to know how Alfetta had figured it out. Stumpf wanted to know what she knew about Lulita's murder. Alfetta just wanted to know when her lawyer was going to show up.

Stumpf broke the silence when he buzzed Connie. "Hi, Connie. Do you think you can find Jacob Plessy, get him in here? We need a little help and… maybe some more help. Thanks."

A six–foot lady with brown hair draped over her maybe hundred–pound frame arrived first. "Alfetta Tonelli," Redding began, "this is Cathy Ferguson, Esquire. She has agreed to take your case. Right Miss Ferguson?" Ferguson shot Redding a sharp look, but relaxed her features when she turned to Alfetta.

She held out her hand to Alfetta, still sitting in the over–crowded room. Stumpf said, "We have some more room down the hall in the lunch, er, meeting room, okay? Everybody?" And they left his office, looking like a clown act climbing out of a VW Beetle.

Redding led the way down the hall, past his office and into the lunch room.

Cathy Ferguson, in her late twenties, knew everyone in the room, but made introductions all around as a formality, trying to put her new client at ease. Then she said, "Gentlemen? I'd like to confer a few minutes with my client," and the detectives left.

She turned to Alfetta and said, "Why are you here?"

Alfetta told her how she was involved in the cigarettes, how scared she was of Tony and his men, how she thought Tony's guys had killed Lulita, how she and Lulita had been working as a team, just to deliver, and how she figured out that Lulita's truck had been hijacked and how Lulita had probably been killed, and how Tony wanted her to set up another run, this time fake, to catch his guys, but if the sting didn't work, how he'd kill her father, then Gino, then her. And that she owed Tony all this money. She said she came to the station to tell everything, but she didn't want to go to prison, and in return she'd tell everything she knew, even about changing the trucks' records.

Cathy Ferguson said, "What kind of deal, exactly, do you have in mind? Did you see all the charges they have against you? And then there's the federal charges; that's another whole basket of snakes."

"I didn't understand the charges," Alfetta said, "and I'm not even connected to some of them. I think they're fishing."

"Certainly they are," Cathy Ferguson said, "but if I get this right, they don't know what you're offering, either. Am I right?" Alfetta nodded. "So what we have here is a whole bowl of nothing, at the moment."

"I'm still arrested," she said.

"But not really; not formally charged," Ferguson said. "They're scaring you. Notice? No handcuffs. You still have your purse, your phone, everything. Don't start worrying yet. What you need to tell me is what you're prepared to do for them—work with Tony, until they get him on the cigarette charges, find out which one of his guys killed Lulita. I mean, you're not arrested at this moment, for real, but you are going to be in one hell of a mess, very little time from now, as soon as the assistant District Attorney shows up and they all get their act together."

"You mean, I can, like, get up and walk out of here?"

"At this moment, yes, but you're better off sitting tight. They'll just come and get you in an hour or two, anyway. And if you make a break for it, they'll suspect a lot more, and you won't be getting deals."

Thunder roared overhead. "That's bad," Alfetta said. "I came here with my top down; it looked like such a nice day. Can I go outside and put my top up, roll up the windows?"

Cathy leaned out into the hallway, where she could see Stumpf's door was open. "Detectives, could you please accompany us to my client's car? Her top is down."

She heard someone use a profanity, then the two detectives emerged and looked at her. Stumpf said, "Let's go." They all went out to the lot and the Miata was saved.

As they came in, a cloudburst caught the last of them, which happened to be Mr. Blackstone himself, Detective Jerry Redding. He got soaked. As they stood in the vestibule, Redding, who had clearly gotten the worst of it, looked down at his sloshy shoes and limp slacks, and said, "Well, at least I got rid of those nasty creases…" It was a joke, but he delivered it so deadpan that no one cracked a smile until he finally did.

They walked back to the lunch room, heard violent thunder, saw a lot of lightning, watched as the lights in the station flickered and then went out. Then, when the generator kicked in, the lights came up and revealed a man about Ferguson's age, height and weight, who couldn't have been any wetter if he had fallen out of a boat.

"Ladies and gentlemen, I present to you Assistant District Attorney Jacob Plessy," said Redding, feeling better, seeing someone suffering more than he was. Then he turned to Plessy and said, "I've got a fresh towel in my locker. Head to the men's room, I'll bring it." He nodded and disappeared around the corner.

Everyone sat around the Masonite–covered table in the lunch room, screeching folding chairs across the concrete floor, to arrange them into natural pairs. Redding soon joined them, wheeling his desk chair in and noticeably not wearing his customary jacket. Or shoes. He parked at the end of the table, Stumpf to his left, both of them close to the door.

Plessy came in a moment later, looking like a Labrador Retriever fresh from the car wash. He apologized for holding everyone up and sat down across from Stumpf, at Redding's right.

It was Stumpf who spoke first. "This murder investigation has led us in some unanticipated directions. We've all met; we know why we're here." He glanced at Plessy, who raised his shoulders and hands in a 'Who, me?' gesture, and Stumpf continued, "ADA Plessy has agreed to join us, to try to sort out some of the jurisdictional complications.

"As you know, I met the husband of the deceased, Daniel Estes, at the Locked & and Safe in Dolton, Illinois this morning. He had discovered the storage space that was unknown to him, but was in his late wife, Lulita's, name.

Because he had the presence of mind to call me, we were able to preserve the scene, with the help of two local police officers. When I arrived, he, the two officers, and the two agents from each of the BATFE and FBI were there, waiting.

"I'm investigating a murder; I didn't need to do too much with the ten pallets of cigarettes we found in the locker. The locals and the feds and I have all agreed to share information. Now, that explains the cigarettes, the feds, and Detective Redding's presence. What isn't clear to me, yet, is why our Alfetta Tonelli here called me to tell me she had some information pertaining to these cigarettes.

"Miss Tonelli's family owns the U–Drive–Em franchise here in town, and specifically the truck in which Lulita Estes's body was found. She started to tell me she knew something about the cigarettes across the state line, and maybe how all this ties together. But then she said she wanted a deal. So that's why all of us are here. Should Alfetta get a deal? What kind of deal? In return for what? She already told me she didn't kill Lulita Estes, and let's say I believe her for now. So, who wants to start? What have we all stepped in?"

Detective Fred Stumpf looked directly at Public Defender Cathy Ferguson, who had her left hand covering Alfetta's right, flat on the table. Alfetta looked back at her, then at Plessy.

Ferguson said, "In all this confusion of the last half hour, I've had very little time to confer with my client. May we have a moment?" Everyone

else walked out into the hall. Plessy, last out, shut
the door.

In the hallway, Stumpf and Redding filled him
in. "So what kind of deal, for which crime, and
for what information?" he asked both detectives,
still bewildered.

"She didn't kill Lulita, I'm pretty sure of that,"
Stumpf said, "So you give her a deal on the
murder. Work that angle. It's a more serious
charge, and she isn't sure that I believe her. She
might spill a lot of information on the cigs. And
since that's federal, we can't do much with that.
Say, Jason, can we even make her a deal on the
federal charges?"

"N-n-n-not really," he said. "But she doesn't
know that. Cathy does, but Alfetta's so shaken
that if we rattle her enough, fast enough, we
might get everything she knows. The murder is
our problem; the cigarettes are ninety percent
federal. Cathy's not going to represent her on
federal charges, anyway; and we're not going to
prosecute on them. But if we can speed up the
pace, we'll know enough to help the feds, and you
can bet they'll want to walk all over our dead lady
in the truck, who probably crossed state lines, one
way or another, that night."

Stumpf clapped softly, once. "Break huddle," he
said. Redding and he started for the lunchroom
door. It took Plessy a moment to get himself in

gear, never having played football, being thinner than a yard line and all. Redding knocked on the door. The men entered.

Everyone sat down, and Cathy Ferguson read from her half–page of notes. "My client wants immunity in any cases involving the cigarettes. She knows she is innocent of the murder. She is prepared to tell you all she knows about the cigarettes. Names, dates, methods—whatever you want—but she doesn't want to go to prison for anything having to do with those cigarettes."

Redding said, "Since I'm leading the cigarette investigation, I'd like to know what all that entails." He looked at Ferguson. "May I ask your client a few questions?"

"Understanding that I may tell her not to answer any or all of them, go ahead."

"Okay. Miss Tonelli, do you know who transported those cigarettes in your trucks?"

"Yes," she said, without looking at her lawyer.

Before Redding could ask another question, Ferguson held up her hand in his direction, signaling STOP, and said to Alfetta, "When he asks you a question, you look at me, to see if you should answer it, before you say anything. Okay? You understand?"

Tonelli nodded. Ferguson addressed Redding. "Okay, go ahead."

Redding looked at Stumpf, then said, "Now, Miss Tonelli, you told the detective you didn't kill

Lulita Estes, right?" Alfetta nodded. "But you know who did, don't you?"

Ferguson stopped Alfetta from answering. Unnecessary, since she wasn't making signs that she would. The defense attorney whispered into Alfetta's ear, and Alfetta nodded. Then Alfetta whispered into the lawyer's ear. Ferguson thought for a moment, then she whispered back. Alfetta nodded again, and Ferguson said, "My client has a hunch, only that. A theory, and before she says anything more, she needs to know that she will not be prosecuted in the murder case."

Stumpf looked at Plessy. "What say you, Counsel for the Prosecution?"

Plessy played his role. "You're asking me to grant immunity to a suspect in a murder case, so your fellow detective can get information on what is at best a tax–evasion case? And we're not even talking about Indiana taxes here. And just a minute ago, didn't your client want immunity from charges related to the cigarettes? So, we're to get information, maybe, on both cases, as long as we don't prosecute Alfetta Tonelli here?"

"That's right, Jacob. I don't think my client killed Lulita, and I don't think she knows exactly who did kill her. But I do believe that the murder and the cigarettes are related, and I do believe that if we get closer to the person or people responsible in the cigarette case, we'll be very close to the murderer or murderers. But it's your call."

Plessy looked at Cathy Ferguson and the lady said, "It's evident that no one here believes my client has anything to do with the murder of Lulita Estes, and she doesn't. So, why don't we get back to talking about a deal on the cigarettes?"

Plessy was looking for their angle. "You'd rather get a pass on cigarettes, and face… whatever on the murder and conspiracy, whatever comes out of the Estes murder investigation?"

Alfetta and her attorney looked at each other. Alfetta squeezed Ferguson's hand. Ferguson said, "My client agrees. No charges in the cigarette cases; whatever happens in the murder case, happens." She looked at Alfetta. "Right?" Alfetta nodded.

Stumpf raised his voice. "Connie, you got everything on tape?"

Connie Clark's voice came over the speaker in the ceiling. "Loud and clear. We're rolling. Just speak normally."

Cathy Ferguson looked at Detective Redding. "That's new, isn't it, Detective?"

Redding replied, "We don't like reading our own handwriting. This works. Besides, you'll get a written copy of everything… Shall we get to it?" Redding stood up, walked slowly around the table, all the time looking at Alfetta. Then he said, "So, tell us all about the cigarettes. Names, dates, how you figured out where they went and why you didn't know. Especially, who you were working for, and was Lulita Estes in it as deep as you?"

Chapter Eleven: Alfetta's story

Alfetta looked at her lawyer, who was still holding her trembling hand. Cathy Ferguson nodded her assurance, and Alfetta began.

"Most of this, you'd figure out anyway, so I'm just going to save you some time. Lulita and I knew each other in grade school. We were friends, but I was a year older. Really good friends, though; we lived only a block apart. Sharonda isn't really an Estes. Her father was Lulita's boyfriend before she married Clarence Nicholson. Sharonda's not mixed; she's black, just like her mommy and daddy. But she doesn't know that. Just before Sharonda was born, Lulita married Nicholson and moved to be with his family, south of Chicago. I didn't see her for, like, fourteen, fifteen years."

"You kept in touch?" Redding asked. "Continue, please. You didn't see Lulita for all that time. How did you keep in touch?"

"We didn't. I was amazed when I got an email from her, out of the blue, just before Christmas last year. We went to the phone right away, talked a while, caught up. Then she said she looked me up on line and saw that I was still in the truck business, and she asked if I could do an old friend a favor. She sounded like she was about to sign me up to sell Amway or something. 'Are you making enough money?' And 'Don't you hate it when your trucks are just sitting, nobody out driving them, making you money?' We drove halfway each to have lunch and talk about it." Redding leaned forward. "What happened at lunch?"

"Well, it was so great to see her. She hadn't changed much since, well, all those years. Of course she told me about Sharonda, and losing Nick—that's who she called her husband--then about meeting Daniel and having Lilly. We talked about the usual stuff, but it gradually got into the conversation, that she was not doing too well financially, that carpentry's kind of spotty work, seasonal, and Daniel liked to show off once in a while. He dressed kinda fancy, liked to wear jewelry. Well, anyway, Lulita told me to meet this guy, Tony. Oh, they weren't having an affair or anything, but, well, she said I had to meet him. And then he walked into the restaurant!"

"Just like that?" Redding said.

"Yeah, just like that." Alfetta thought a few seconds. "Seemed like one big ol' coincidence to me, too. But how lucky, you know? We were giddy—does anybody still say 'giddy?' We were giddy from seeing each other, and we'd each had a drink. Just one. Anyway, here's this Tony guy…"

"What's Tony's last name?"

"Oh, I didn't find that out until later, but it's Gemelli, like the pasta."

"That his real name?"

"I don't know. It's the name Lulita told me. Anyway, may I continue?" Redding nodded. "So this Tony, he has this business, distribution, in Chicago. Legal stuff, mostly, but discounted."

"Discounted?" Plessy hadn't said a word for a long time. Maybe he was drying out.

"Yes, 'discounted.' Like, cigarettes are twice as expensive in Chicago as in Indiana, because taxes. So, like Tony buys cigarettes in bulk from a friend in Indiana, pays almost full price, all legit so far. Then he brings them into Illinois, and he has six or seven stores that sell them to particular customers. He sells to some big–shot restaurant or night club, too. I don't know who that is."

"Do you know his other customers?"

"No, nobody. My part of this was to get the truck for Lulita to drive. She'd make a run to his storage place in Indiana someplace and pick up the cigarettes. Tony had his guys there to load, and a couple other guys at the other end, to unload."

"Who's 'his guys'?"

"I don't know. She said they were Mexicans, never talked to her. They didn't let her get out of the truck, either, to load or unload. She'd just sit, play the radio, take a nap. They had all the equipment at both places. It never went into the trucks."

Redding stood up, paced around the table again. He said, "Connie, you getting this?" and got a double–click on the speaker, the code for affirmative. "Those 'guys,'" he said, "always the same ones?"

"I don't know for sure. I never asked her, but Lulita did say she felt safe with them, so that sounds like she was getting used to the same guys."

"They always go to the same place for pickup and dropoff?"

"Pickup, yes. Lulita told me, but I didn't pay attention. I wrote it down on the first run. Don't remember… Some place in Michigan City. And I thought she always delivered to the same place, but this last run was different."

"She tell you that?"

"She called me from the truck. They had a new place to take them and she wanted me to know, because the mileage was going to be different. It was, too. And that's how I found Locked & Safe. She was supposed to be going to Storage King, but she got diverted."

Stumpf, who had been quiet all along, said, "I'd be interested to know how you found Locked & and Safe. And do you think she was looking for help—that she knew she was getting hijacked?"

Redding hushed him and said, "We'll certainly go over that with you in detail; I'd like to know, too. But for now, please tell me how you accounted for the mileage."

"That's what takes most of my time, actually," Alfetta said. "Every time Lulita took a truck out, it would come back with, you know, mileage to Chicago and back. About two hundred miles. Then I'd have to go back through the truck's records and bury those extra miles in other trips, 'maintenance,' and wherever I could. Daddy's the only other person who ever looks at these records, and he's mostly concerned with maintenance items, the price of gas, and, I mean, he's retiring, retired officially, so he's just not there much. As long as everything adds up okay, he doesn't pay a lot of attention."

Stumpf again wanted to know, "Don't you run into trouble, reconciling the cameras? I mean, when the truck is gone and it's supposedly sitting in the lot; doesn't that show up on camera?"

"Sure, but in a week, the record is overwritten. But the trucks go out on the nights when I'm working; it's not too hard to have things go wrong with cameras or the recorder. And you already know about that bird, made the nest right on top of the camera, her tail hangs down in front of the lens."

Stumpf nodded. "Sometimes," she said, "there is such a thing as luck."

"One more thing for now," Redding said. "Money. How did you get paid, and where's the money? And—you didn't go shopping for cigarettes, right? Did he, or did he have you pick up and pay?"

"That was complicated, but all we did, really, was pick up and drop off. And we got paid. He didn't want the sellers to know who we were."

"Why would he trust Lulita with so much valuable cargo? He hardly knew her."

"Okay, fine. He trusted Lulita because she had two children and a husband she loved. He had that over her head. The Mexicans? I don't know what he had on the Mexicans. They could have disappeared at any time. But he kept them loyal, paid them in cash. Well, he had Lulita do it. That's what I gathered."

"'Gathered?'" Stumpf asked. "She told you?"

"Well, I don't know. Maybe she told me or maybe that's just what I've come to believe. I—I really can't remember how come I thought it was cash. But it's what I think I remember, anyway."

"Go on."

"I can't say for sure that I ever heard that Tony and the Mexicans actually met. Maybe he hired them through a middleman, some kind of home–grown employment service or something." She laughed. "You know what I mean. Some guy who managed the labor."

"And how did you get paid?"

"Lulita and I had a special account, in her name, in Chicago. She put all our money in that."

"You trusted her?"

"Of course, I trusted her. She paid me every time I asked."

"You ever see the paperwork for this account?"

"No, but she had to have it. Her husband was always short of money. If she put it in their regular bank account, he'd see it."

Redding pushed back from the table, his desk chair going too far. He hit the wall. Not hard, but not cool. He scooched back to his place. "Just how much was he paying you and Lulita?"

"Lulita got six thousand dollars for each trip," Alfetta said, "and I got ten for including the truck."

"And you just started doing this in December?"

"January."

Redding asked, "How many trips, total?"

"Ten," Alfetta said. Then, "No, eleven. We made a van run in January, more like training, two pallets of cigarettes. We got half pay for that, too."

"So," Redding said, "you got…" he gazed at the ceiling, "a hundred and five thousand, total, and Lulita got sixty–three? Would that be right? And all that money would be in some bank account Lulita had, and you trusted her."

"Yes, right. And I did."

Redding and Stumpf exchanged a look. Alfetta said, "What?"

Redding glanced at Stumpf. "Go ahead."

Stumpf said, "Daniel Estes discovered a bank account he didn't know about, and a safe deposit box. There was ninety–six thousand dollars in the new account, but nothing but paper—birth certificates, car titles, and stuff—he took us there. That's what was in the safe deposit box. Somebody's seventy–six thousand dollars short. You said she gave you money, the one time you asked. How much was that?"

"Ten thousand."

Redding stood up. "Math gives me a headache," he said. "Can we all be back here at nine o'clock tomorrow morning, fresh," he looked at Plessy, "and dry, ready to think and remember stuff?" The meeting adjourned.

Redding followed Stumpf into his office. He closed the door and looked at Stumpf, said, "As they say in psychiatry school, 'This ain't right.'"

"Serious, Jerry? I mean, I've never heard you use language like that. 'Ain't,' indeed. And you went to psychiatry school?"

Jerry just looked down as Fred continued. "And you're right. No matter how sloppy our math may be, there's a lot of money missing.

Chapter Twelve: Breaking bad backfires.

Daniel Estes kept going through Lulita's things, still trying to find out more about who this 'Toni' was, when he decided to explore her purse. Her wallet wasn't in there. He gave that to Stumpf, already. The wallet, that's business; the purse, that's personal. Guys are trained from the moment they can crawl that purses are off–limits, sacred sanctuaries where males are never allowed. Somewhere, there's a university study that concluded a major reason guys go transvestite is so they can have a purse that they're allowed to get into.

But women, in similar studies, seldom know what's in their purses. No, not the fancy, tiny, going–to–the–opera purses they pull out of the closet once every three years, for some special event. The day–to–day purses, the size of shopping bags, that they lug everywhere, just in case there's—what?—an unannounced apocalypse. That's the purse Daniel was looking into.

Crumpled tissue, lipstick, a pencil and some pens, a few scraps of paper with notes on them—he'd get to those, later. Then he flattened out and sorted some wadded–up receipts, went through business cards, a few peanuts and a french fry, seventy–three cents in spare change, some samples of cologne in spray bottles that held about a drop, a couple tampons, a handkerchief, a little bottle of hand sanitizer, a compact with powder and a mirror and one of those little round pads, a comb, earbuds, sunglasses, some grit—either sand or maybe salt from the french fry, he couldn't tell.

It was only after all this had been dumped on the bed and sorted, and while he was putting it back, that he noticed a stiff spot in the wall of the purse, stiff because there was a pocket there, and in the pocket, an old, small iPhone.

This time, Estes didn't start sleuthing on his own. He gingerly put it in a plastic bag and zipped it up, then called Detective Stumpf. "I don't know if it's something," he said, "or nothing. But it was in her purse and I didn't know she had it; I've never seen it… Sir, it's a hundred miles… Yes, I'll bring it in… No, I don't know about the charger. I'll look, but okay, I won't charge it or anything. It'll be just like I found it. I learned my lesson at the Locked & and Safe." And he drove into Indiana again.

Stumpf didn't care that it was Sunday. *Goes with the job. Plus, this is big. Or at least it could be. Glad that dilly didn't try to check it, could have erased something or maybe got it to lock itself up. Artie's going to have fun with this in the lab. He's perfect for this.*

Artie English was twenty–three, five–six, and chubby, the tech in the crime lab. Bright, enthusiastic, and as naïve a nerd as walked the

Earth. His technical skills and his pride in pleasing his boss were his life. Even his hobby—he had a hobby, not a girlfriend—was studying what he called, "ancient forensics," meaning whatever was done before there was a computer on every desk, when phones were for just talking on and had wires attached, and when airbags in cars were optional. Forensics from before he was born, in other words.

Estes rang the bell, and Stumpf let him in. He was surprised to see two girls with him. "This is Sharonda," he said, "and this," the one resting her butt on his forearm, "is Lilly." He looked at Sharonda. "Say hello to Detective Stumpf."

Stumpf tipped his imaginary hat to Sharonda and gave a little bow. Estes held his breath—he never knew what his fifteen–year–old rebellious sophomore would do. Then he gulped air as she smiled, curtsied, and said, "Pleased to meet you, Officer."

Stumpf started to say, "Detective," but bit his tongue, recovered quickly, and said, with a theatrical bow, "The pleasure is all mine, Miss." Then he turned to Lilly, who turned her head away, hiding her face behind her daddy's ear.

"Let's go into the lunchroom," he said. "Anybody need the bathroom? It's just past here," and he turned right, pulled out a chair halfway down the long table, and sat down.

Daniel and Lilly went to freshen up. Sharonda went to the chair just past Stumpf's, nodded in its direction, and asked, "Is this seat taken?" and, when the detective assured her it wasn't, sat down next to him, making him uncomfortable.

That's not how teenagers act. Not this side of the old movies, anyway. Maybe this one's different? She's up to something. Is this show for me or her father? Then he paused. *Either way, at least she's behaving. Yeah, she's up to something; it won't take long to find out what.* "Sharonda, right?" When she smiled, he said, matching her formal character, "Would you care for a chilled beverage?"

She said, "Thank you. I would be delighted."

Stumpf got her a Diet Pepsi, the only drink in the often–empty machine. Daniel came in, Lilly walking, holding his left hand. Lulita's purse was in his right. He sat the toddler down, her chin about level with the tabletop.

"Sorry we don't have any booster chairs," Stumpf said. Sharonda said nothing, but stood up and walked over to her little sister, picked her up, returned to her seat, and put the little girl on her lap.

"You grownups talk," she said, diverting Lilly's attention.

Estes and Stumpf exchanged glances; Estes shrugged, and pulled the iPhone out of his pocket, still in the bag. He pushed it across the table.

Stumpf said, "This was Lulita's? You found it in her purse, the purse you've gone all through and just now thought to bring in?"

"Sorry, Detective," he said. "Guilty. Sorry about the purse. But everything's in there, I mean, except the phone here and her wallet, that I already gave you. I didn't go into that at all, either."

Stumpf scowled. Estes continued, "The phone was in her purse; I never saw it before, and I never saw an iPhone charger in the house. We all have Androids."

"Both of you?"

Estes nodded at Sharonda. "All three of us. We don't have, never had iPhones."

Sharonda was playing with Lilly, and she didn't look up as she said, "Mom always charged hers in the car. The cord's probably under the passenger seat."

Estes shot a look at his daughter. "You knew about this phone?" She nodded. He leaned over the table and raised his voice. "How long have you known about this?" She shrank away.

Stumpf took over, looked at her with his most–avuncular expression. She didn't appear frightened. Stumpf looked at her father, said, "I'll be the detective today, Mr. Estes." Estes sat down as Stumpf turned to Sharonda, who was Mona Lisa–smiling, and said, "Sharonda, how long has your mother had this phone?"

"Since winter, I guess. It's kinda new, but it's an old, real old model. Like, two models ago. New to her, I mean."

"When was the first time you remember seeing it?"

"Some time last winter, when it was real cold."

"Before Christmas?"

She hesitated. Lilly was squirming. "No, I don't think so. No."

Stumpf motioned for Sharonda to move Lilly. She put the little girl on the table, rested her hand on Lilly's leg, both to calm her and to keep track of her. Then he continued with Sharonda, "Did you ever see her talk on it? Do you know who she talked to on it? Ever hear what she said?"

"She talked to her girlfriends, I guess."

"Who? Did you ever meet them?"

"No, I didn't know them. They were her new friends. One was somebody named Toni. I think another one was, began with an A, Alanis or something. I always thought Tony was a boy's name. But I looked it up. There was even some hair care things, brand Toni, so I guess it was Tony, but with an 'i.'"

"Did you ever hear what they talked about?"

"No, not really. I didn't pay attention. I think they smoked. Mom didn't smoke, but I remember she talked a lot about cigarettes." She looked at her father. "Mom didn't smoke, and neither do I," she said. "I swear."

Estes calmly said, "I know, sweetie. Just keep on talking to the Detective. I'm listening. I didn't know you and your mother had so many secrets."

"Daddy, we didn't 'have secrets.' I didn't care about what Mom was talking about, or who her friends were. I don't pay attention to what you and Mom do. Er, did."

Estes got up, walked around the table, looked at his older daughter. He picked Lilly off the table.

And Sharonda shut her mouth tight as the door to Fort Knox, crossed her arms in front of her, and leaned back in her chair. Silence, awkward and stringent, held forth as Stumpf made notes.

Stumpf flipped a new page on his notebook while he looked at Estes. Lilly had fallen asleep in his arms, and was drooling on his shirt. Estes looked at the spot and saw that Stumpf had already noticed. "Kids are great," he said. Stumpf nodded. Sharonda was pacing at the end of the room, occasionally looking out the window, arms still locked across her chest.

Stumpf said, "Okay, when and where did you find this?" holding up the baggie with the phone in it.

"About two minutes before I called you."

"You were going through her purse, the purse you couldn't find, earlier?"

"I—I'm sorry. When I found it, I just wanted to look through…"

"Forget the purse for now. Damage done. The phone—you didn't turn it on?"

"No, I didn't. I immediately set it down on the bed, went and got that Ziplock bag, and put it in. Then I called you. I didn't try to turn it on; I hardly looked at it, in fact."

"Well, Mr. Estes, thank you for that. And thank you for coming over right away, and introducing me to your family." He looked at Sharonda, who took a moment from looking out the window to glance at him over her shoulder, then turned back, her arms still crossed. "I can't do anything with this," he held up the phone, "until tomorrow, when the lab is open, but I really appreciate your coming all this way, on a Sunday."

"Sure, Detective. I'm going back to work tomorrow; there's no other time to do it. But you've got everything that I know of, that's at all interesting." He headed for the door, and Sharonda swung around the table to catch up, looking at Stumpf like she wanted to say something, but she kept going. Stumpf let them out.

Chapter Thirteen:
Estes examines his soul.

It's been a week. Where's the interrogation?

On the forty–minute drive back to Dolton, Lilly slept in her car seat in the back, and Sharonda rode shotgun. Estes wanted to ask her so many things, things like how did she know her mother so well, and why didn't he? "Kiddle," he said, "why didn't you tell me Mom had that extra phone?"

She looked at him but rolled her eyes before answering. "Why would I? I never really paid attention. So Mom has another phone, so what? Why would I tell you? Would you care?"

He was angry at her tone, but angrier with himself for asking the dumb question. "I'm just upset," he said. "I don't know why I would have expected you to think anything of it, one way or another. I'm just… looking…"

"For anything that takes away your guilt?" Estes pulled to the shoulder of the road, hitting the brakes hard. "What, exactly *what*, do you mean by that? I loved your mother! You little…" He looked for a word, couldn't find one, and left the echoes to die down as Lilly started to cry. The traffic rattled by at sixty miles an hour, just a foot or two from his door handle.

He looked in the rearview mirror, put the car in gear and nailed the gas, spraying gravel from the screaming right rear tire, taking years off the tread as they merged back into the lane. *Calm down, Daniel. She's just a kid. Doesn't notice much. She's lashing out. Her mother was murdered. She's uncomfortable being questioned. Why would she think it was anything she ought to tell me? I'm not her real dad; she's told me that often enough. She's a kid. She's hurting, too. She doesn't know anything.* And he kept driving in silence.

He stopped at McDonald's but they didn't get out of the car. They were almost home. Lilly woke up at the smell of french fries, and Sharonda was as hungry as her stepdad was, so when they got home five minutes later, they all rushed to the table and opened the bags. Sharonda went to the fridge, got milk out for Lilly and a can of diet for herself. Without asking, she brought her stepdad a beer.

He didn't really want a beer, but he appreciated the gesture. "Thanks, Kiddle," he said. "Been a rough day."

"Yeah, Daddy, it has. A rough week." She dipped another fry in the puddle of ketchup she'd poured on one of the burger wrappers. "So Nana's coming over tomorrow? Is Gumpa coming with her?"

"They're both coming tomorrow, before you go to school," Estes said. "They'll be here while we're both gone; then it's up to you to take care of Lilly until I get home. They'll be taking turns watching Lilly for a while, until we figure out what to do. And with school almost over…"

"You're going to make me into Lilly's full–time, live–in babysitter all summer! Daddy, that's not *fair*. I'll go crazy. None of my friends…"

"Sharonda, we all have to come together, do extra. I'll be working longer—it's summer. There's longer daylight and more work to do, but we'll all live through this. We have to." He looked into her red, despairing eyes, "We have to help each other."

"I know, Daddy. It's just that, well, it's summer, and I…" She cried. "I would like to go to my room now." And she left, but not before dipping one more french fry, which she took with her.

Lilly had been watching all this in silence, slapping a pickle slice on her forehead and licking it, then wiping it on the bridge of her nose and licking it again. Estes took it away from her and tried to give her what was left of the burger patty that she had ripped to pieces while he and her sister were talking. So she cried.

Lord, what a mess I've made. Sharonda needs me, but she acts like she hates me even more. Lilly. Oh, what can I do with this little baby girl? She's missing Mommy, but she doesn't get it that Mommy's not coming back. And she's got to get used to Nana every day… And Nana's going to have to get used to me, and me, her. At least she's not going to make Lilly pay for my sins.

He washed Lilly and put her to bed, cleaned up the kitchen table, pulled off his shoes, and collapsed onto his bed. Checked the alarm—

six–thirty. He pulled off his clothes and put his
head on his pillow. Daniel Estes wanted to go to
sleep, but he didn't. Couldn't.

*What have I done? Poor Lulita. All she wanted
to do was help out the family. Or maybe put away
a secret stash and run off somewhere. Or surprise
us all at Christmas. Yeah, right.* He was getting
angry. Tried, but he couldn't fight it. *What the hell
was she doing with that Toni and that cokehead
friend of hers?*

Estes went over that night, a little over a week
ago, when Lulita had come home at two a.m.,
tired and with no explanation of where she'd been

*Out with her girlfriends, she said. Shopping, she
said. At two in the morning? What the hell? And
why didn't she just tell me? I can handle it. Yeah,
sure, it's wrong. Stealing is wrong, but her heart
was in the right place. Probably.*

He re–examined that night in his memory. He
was awake, making a sandwich. She wasn't home,
wasn't answering her phone. Voicemail. *What the
hell am I supposed to leave on voicemail? 'Hi, it's
one o'clock and I'm wondering where you and
your girlfriends are shopping. Saint freaking
Louis, maybe?'*

So when she came home that night, he tried to
ask her. They kept their voices down, kids' sleeping
and all, but the intensity was there. She told him
about Alfetta, tried to tell him Toni was another
girlfriend, changed her story from 'shopping' to

'helping Toni move, with Alfetta's truck—lucky she has that rental place.'

Daniel didn't buy it. *She was flat–out lying. She knew I knew it, but she still wouldn't tell me what the hell was going on! Treating me like a stupid kid, like I wasn't able to survive knowing the truth. She even said it: "You can't handle the truth," like she's Jack Nicklaus… Jack Nicholson. God, I'm tired.*

As her evasions grew more obvious and implausible, his frustrations grew with them. *She couldn't tell me anything. Who's this Alfetta— that's her name, Alfetta, like the little car. Who's this Alfetta? Some girl from school, hadn't heard from her in forever, now they're friends again, and she had to help her move some other girl named Toni, with her own truck? At midnight? Yeah, I believe that. And then Toni's just another friend, there to help out.*

Estes was torturing himself, going over the night. Over and over, like he had done each night since… since that night, when they were standing there, nose to nose, arguing in whisper–shouts, when her phone buzzed in her purse. At two a.m. "Answer it!" he growled.

"No," she said. "It's nobody, and besides, I don't know where my phone is."

Her purse was on the floor, separating her tennis shoes from his bare feet.

"Down there," he said.

"It will stop," she said. "And I still can't tell where it is."

There's a light in the kitchen; there's a light in the hall. Why? Why would she lie? I could see her purse. She could see her purse.

Daniel said, "Right there, at your damn feet!" and he grabbed the back of her head, almost playfully, and started to push her head down, to look at the purse.

She resisted, said, "I can't see it," and the man who made his living swinging a hammer slammed her head down.

"There!" he spat out the word as her chin hit her breastbone. He heard the snap. It sounded like someone broke a baseball bat, hitting a fastball on the letters. But there was no clatter of wood splinters' hitting the ground, only a little puff of air from his wife's lips as she started to crumple to the floor, and a single yap from Augie. He didn't even hear the dog.

He caught her limp body as her head rolled back. She was looking at him, not speaking, but she was looking at him. "Daniel?" she mouthed, but there was no sound, and she collapsed fully into his arms as he fell backwards, she on top of him, eyes still looking at his. But there was no spirit behind her eyes. The windows to the soul stayed open, but they saw nothing.

Augie, likely surprised by the sound of the snap and irritated by the commotion in the house while he was trying to sleep, came around the corner, looked at the couple, and let out a half-hearted yap, but Daniel shot him a look, and the little dog let out a faint whimper and slunk back out of sight.

Frantic, Daniel tried to think. *Call 911? And tell them what—that I just killed my wife? No, I've got to get her out of here. First things first. Where? In the freezer, in the garage. No—we left that freezer in the old house.*

Got to hide her, move her away, somewhere! Where? Who was that friend, the one that's an Italian car? Alfetta? Has a truck rental, where, where? Indiana, where? Lulita, where? Twelve and twenty, near there somewhere. Get her in the car, Daniel. Think of where you're going, later.

He put socks over his hands—couldn't find gloves—and got his wife's body into a big black leaf bag from a pile of yard equipment and tools in the garage, then hefted her into the trunk of their old Buick. He pulled out of the garage, then had a crazy thought, and he ran back into the kitchen and grabbed his sandwich. He got into the car, backed down the driveway and closed the garage door with the remote, and headed to the Interstate as the Garmin came to life.

I hope this fifty–buck GPS has a database in it. Rentals… Michigan City. Okay, near there, then. He nearly sideswiped a parked car and gave up on the GPS. "Okay, Google. Find truck rentals in Michigan City, Indiana." *Crap. There's a bunch. Twelve and twenty are both east–west. What intersection? Hell, there's one where they almost touch. U–Drive–Em. Let's hope that Alfetta can handle a surprise.*

Daniel Estes drove frantically but on the speed limit and found the U–Drive–Em. He still had no plan; *just hide Lulita's body.* He pulled slowly into the lot, around back. He backed up next to a twenty–foot box truck, the one—and he had no way of knowing, even if he had cared—that was booked to take Josh Terwilliger to Texas later that morning.

He opened the trunk and looked in the bag, half–expecting to see Lulita perk up and smile, but her lifeless eyes gave no hint of recognition.

He opened the back of the truck, went back to the Buick and picked Lulita up, placed her on the floor of the truck, started to close the door, and stopped.

Right there, he said a little prayer of contrition. *I can't leave her there, like that.* So he climbed into the truck, picked her up, and carried her to the front of the dark box. But he misjudged the distance, slammed against the wall at the edge of the dance floor, and unceremoniously dropped the body of his wife up and onto the dance floor, where it skidded until it stopped, all the way up at the front.

He ran to the back of the truck and pulled down the door, wiped off the handle with his shirttail, and latched it, again keeping his prints off the latch handle with his shirt.

He went back to the Buick, moved the trunk lid down until it clicked, slid in behind the wheel, and went home. He was back in bed just in time to hear his alarm go off.

What have I done? He again asked himself, as he fell into sleep, knowing that tomorrow he'd be back at work, Sharonda would be back at school and Gumpy and Nana would be coming over to take care of Lilly…

Chapter Fourteen: The new normal

James and Mary—Gumpy and Nana—arrived at seven–thirty, hugged their son in law, and went into the kitchen where Sharonda was making her own lunch. Three little bags of chips, a peanut butter sandwich, and some grapes in a ziplock bag. She grabbed a box of juice from the pantry, humming something, matching the tune her earbuds blasted into her head, unaware of her grandparents, who had sat down on a couple bar stools at the kitchen island to watch the show.

Sharonda turned around, shrieked, and nearly fell over. Nana and Gumpy ran to her, one on each side, to steady her, but she was fine, and now she was laughing so hard she nearly fell again.

Daniel walked into this scene, saw everyone laughing, and turned around, leaving whatever he was going to say unsaid and immediately forgotten. The trio laughed some more. Augie looked up when Sharonda let loose, looked around, put his head back down.

"Did you get your breakfast, Sharonda?" Nana asked.

"I made eggs for me and Daniel," she said, "and some toast. Coffee, too, but I don't think I did it right. He hated it." She smiled. "So did I."

"Well," Gumpy said, "don't worry about coffee just yet. Somebody your age doesn't need it, and it'll just turn your teeth brown, anyway."

"Yuk," Sharonda said, and started to turn away.

Gumpy tapped her lightly on the arm and said, "But did you make a whole pot? Nana and I love coffee."

Sharonda smiled. "In fact…" and she pointed to a fancy–looking coffee maker with a stainless steel carafe that was sitting on the corner of the counter, under the spice rack. "I have to go to school now," she said. "Thanks for coming to watch Lilly. I love you." Then she ran out the door.

James took two cups from the cabinet and poured from the carafe. The coffee looked dark, but he handed a cup to Mary. They clicked coffee cups as if to toast each other, and each took a healthy sip. And they both spit the vile liquid into the sink, looked at each other, and laughed again.

"Want to try another pot?" Nana said, as Daniel came back into the kitchen.

"You must have tried Sharonda's coffee," he said, noticing Nana with the coffee filter and grinder out on the counter. His in-laws smiled. "Mary, she's learning, but I really don't want her drinking coffee yet, and the way she makes it, I think she's going to put it off a few more years."

He hugged Lulita's parents. "Thank you so much for coming. I don't know what I'd do without you." His voice started to crack as he said, "without you."

"You have us as long as we're on this planet, son," his father said. And he smiled. "Just don't take advantage."

Nana didn't see the twinkle in his eye, but she knew his mischievous tone of voice, and slapped him on the shoulder. "We love it when you take advantage, Daniel," she said. "And if not now, when?" They all hugged again and she said, "Do you pack a lunch? I could make you one for the road."

"Thanks, Mary, but the guys planned something special for me today. Tomorrow, though, for sure. Thanks. I love you both so much." And he was gone.

Lilly was crying as she toddled into the kitchen, wiping her eyes and stinking up the place. Mary nodded toward the smelly toddler and said, "Well, James, if you want me to make coffee, you're first up."

James walked the crying little girl down the hall to the bathroom.

The day was alternately quiet and hectic. Lilly wasn't particularly bothersome, but she required constant vigilance; the kid could climb, and she still seemed intent on learning about things through her sense of taste rather than sight or touch or smell. And she got into the vacuum cleaner attachments in the closet, clever and quick as a monkey. She was sucking on one of the vacuum cleaner's brushes when Nana caught up to her.

Eventually, the grandparents opened up the hide–a–bed sofa in the living room, turned on the television, and laid down with Lilly between them, Augie curled up on the floor in the corner.

They were all asleep there, a rerun of *Gunsmoke* running in black and white, when Sharonda came home. Nana heard her come in, sat up, brushed the sleep from her eyes. She looked at Sharonda, nodded to Lilly, and put her finger to her lips. "Shhh." Sharonda smiled and waved, then headed to her room.

Up in her room, she plugged in her tablet and opened her secret Facebook page. She had two Facebook pages. One was the one her parents monitored; this was the other one, SharShar2004, where she talked with her friends, put up her "good" selfies, gossiped about her boyfriend, her girlfriends' boyfriends, which teachers were mean, what tests were coming up and did anyone have last year's tests, who just got what car for his or her birthday—all the juicy stuff.

As SharShar2004, Sharonda was uninhibited. She told the truth here, as well as the truth as she imagined it and the truth as she wished it were. Her fantasies, in other words, and they blended

seamlessly with the truth and part–truth,
undifferentiated on her blog.

> Well, back to school today. Thanks all
> you guys for the nice things you said
> about my Mom. It's all appreciated.
> Nana and Gumpy are here with Lilly,
> and Dad's back at work. He's not all
> right yet. Very uptight. Not getting it
> that Mom's not here. Lilly doesn't get
> it, either. Augie's really messed up.
> He just lies around all day, doesn't
> know that Mom's not coming back.
> He doesn't even bark at stuff any
> more.
> I think I'm going to be OK some day,
> but not yet. But I'll get used to it, I
> guess. Just hope the killer confesses.
> I KNOW WHO YOU ARE, MURDERER.
> One day, I'll tell the world, too.

She closed the page and turned to her homework.

Nana and Gumpy were awake now, and as they
stirred, Lilly woke up. She was soaked in sweat,
wet, and grumpy. Gumpy's turn. He took the little
girl to the bathroom to get her cleaned up, as
Nana started dinner. Snacks first. Peanut butter on
crackers, peanut butter in celery for dessert.

"Sharonda, if you're hungry, I've got some snacks for you," she shouted to the air. Sharonda and Gumpy magically appeared.

Gumpy helped himself to a napkin and a couple crackers, grunted at little Lilly, who had followed him, and walked to the hide–a–bed. He set down the napkin and folded up the bed, sat down and offered a bite of the cracker to Lilly. She gummed it a little before she pushed it far enough into her mouth to start chewing, smiling the whole time, as Gumpy woofed down a second one and fished around on the end table without looking until he found the remote.

Bonanza was on now, and Ben Cartwright was going to get his heart broken by a beautiful widow lady who just couldn't get over being a widow. *She's like, ninety now, if she's even alive,* James said to himself. He changed to the all-news channel, where some politician was saying something nasty about some other politician, and the talking heads were debating whether it was nasty enough, or just out of line, and apparently it was both, since nobody changed anybody else's mind. Or maybe it was neither.

Sharonda stuffed a celery stick into her mouth and grabbed three crackers, made a triple–decker out of them, and managed to say, "Thanks, Nana," as she turned and headed back to her room. Mary put all the surviving snacks on one plate and brought it out to the TV, where James and Lilly were making faces at each other, the news turned down to where nobody could hear the angry people who were calling each other "my friend," as they said awful things about each others' favorite politicians.

"Why do you watch that stuff, James?" she asked. "They never change their minds. They never come to agreement. They never say anything, except how bad the other guy is, or how the one before that was even worse. It's affecting your digestion and it's making you grumpy… Gumpy."

He handed her the remote. "You choose," he said. "I don't care. They're all a bunch of crooks and liars, as far as I can tell."

"My dear Mr. Sunshine," she said, as she shut off the box.

Daniel came home just after seven, kissed Mary hello, greeted Gumpy. He said he'd ask how their day went, as soon as he took a shower. Five minutes later, barefoot and wearing a white robe, he returned to the living room, where his dinner, microwaved back to life, was on a low table in front of the sofa. "Thanks, Mary," he said, as he dove in. "Thanks for dinner. Thanks for watching Lilly, for being here for Sharonda, for everything."

He looked at Gumpy. "And James, thanks. I don't know what we'd do without you."

"Well, Danny," he said, "we don't, either." He exchanged smiles with Daniel and Mary, "but this I can tell you: it would be expensive."

They laughed as he dug into his dinner again.

Daniel looked around the room. It was small, as living rooms go. Beige carpet that he and Lulita always hated, white walls with a perceptible stripe about waist–high, dirt from peoples' hands, as they leaned on it or as they drew the old wood chairs along it. The dining–room table that Lulita set for Sunday dinner each week, but that was otherwise a repository for unopened mail, a bookbag or purse or a pair of gloves or a hat when it was winter.

The chairs, four of them, one with a booster seat for Lilly and one chair each for Sharonda, himself, and Lulita, the last one to remain forever empty. *It just doesn't seem normal any more. Would it ever be normal again?*

Nana read his thoughts. She walked around behind him, put her hands on his shoulders. "It's going to take a long time," she said. "Forever. But you *will* heal." She let go, turned around, nearly stepped on Augie. "But you, little guy," she said, "you'll just be sad." She walked back to her place, saying to nobody in particular, "We'll all be sad together."

James looked over. "In time, you will get used to it," he said. "But no, you'll never get over it."

He leaned over, put his hand on Daniel's strong arm, looked into his eyes, then dropped his gaze. "Do you want to tell us anything? Do you want to talk about Lulita?"

Daniel just shook his head, finished his dinner, and bussed his plate and silverware to the kitchen. He came back out, hugged both Lulita's parents, and said, "Thank you both so much. Thank you again." His head hung low and his steps dragged as he walked to the bedroom at the end of the hall, and into their bedroom.

Chapter Fifteen:
Nana's an accidental spy.

Sharonda's summer school started much as her sophome year had ended. Nana and Gumpy were back from a two-week's rest, looking forward to less stress, now that they knew where everything was, what the kids liked for dinner; and bedtimes were normalized from the more–casual routine of summer.

Daniel left at dawn, returned around seven, sweaty and tired, hungry and grateful.

Sharonda spent her time in her room; she didn't want to talk about school, other kids, or especially homework. She kept her door closed and she was quiet, so nobody bothered her. "No sense whacking on the hornets' nest, if they're minding their own business," Gumpy said.

Lilly enjoyed having two adults to play with, to wrap around her little fingers, but she slept a lot and wasn't much bother.

Nana and Gumpy watched a lot of television, and they spent hours each day on the old laptop that was once Sharonda's, then Lulita's, learning how to manipulate Facebook, looking for friends they hadn't thought of in decades, researching ancestry, and finding out things that were going on in the scandal–stained halls of Hollywood and D.C., Nana preferring the former and Gumpy, the latter.

Nana was on Facebook when she was asked to sign in. She recognized the names in the menu, but didn't know who SharShar2004 was, and curiosity got the best of her. Sharonda had left the password turned on, and Nana got an eyeful.

Language she couldn't imagine children, let alone Sharonda, would use! And the photos were borderline pornographic, and of boys, too!

Her first instinct was to escape out of there and never look back. But that instinct lasted only a moment, and Mary started reading Sharonda's thoughts. Sad thoughts, funny thoughts, some really silly ideas. The thoughts were as refreshing as they were horrifying.

Refreshing, too—no mention of politics, finances, taxes, adult worries; anyone over seventeen was ancient, and anyone under fourteen or so, irrelevant. Sure, there were singers, cable, and movie stars, and fashion, or what passed for it. And which of her friends were fun, cool, sometimes morons…

And there was this one passage: I KNOW WHO YOU ARE, MURDERER. Mary logged out, logged back into her own identity, and closed the laptop. She was shaking, wondering if this was just another high–schooler's fantasy, or did Sharonda know something?

"James," she said, as they spooned in the bed. "I'm worried about Sharonda."

"She's a teenager. You should be worried about her."

"No, seriously, James. She said something on her Facebook page, her secret Facebook page."

James was coming back into full consciousness. "She has a secret Facebook page? How did you find it?"

"I don't know, exactly. I was trying to get onto my page, and it gave me this choice of accounts, and there was this one I didn't recognize, SharShar something, so I logged in."

"Mary?"

"I know, I know. I shouldn't. But it was innocent enough. Well, no, it wasn't. But I'm trying to tell you that I saw something that really bothered me in there."

"She likes boys?" Nana shook her head, started to speak. "She likes *girls?*"

"No, James. Just shut up. She said she knows who the murderer is, and she's going to spill the beans some day!"

"Oh, Mary," he said. "She's just spouting off. She's been to the detective; she could tell us; she could tell her own father…"

"What if she's scared? Maybe she's taunting the murderer, hoping he'll give himself up, rather than get exposed by…"

"By a fifteen–year–old girl? Look, Mary, she's putting this on, what, her 'secret' Facebook page? You don't think the police have already been there? Daniel gave them permission to go through all that stuff, gave them the passwords, everything."

"Daniel doesn't know about this account."

"How can you be so sure he doesn't know about it?"

So she told him what she saw. James agreed, said maybe they should tell Daniel in the morning.

Daniel Estes was running late the next morning; there was no time to tell him about Sharonda's secret Facebook account, and he wouldn't have been able to do anything about it all day at work, anyway.

After Sharonda went to school and Gumpy and Nana had their breakfasts, Mary pulled out the laptop.

"You're sure this is Sharonda's account?" Gumpy asked. He read over the posts, some language; he saw the photos. He shook his head. "SharShar," he said, "there's a lot that you're not telling us."

Then he came to the "I know who you are" quote. His eyes opened wide as he read it over. Twice. "No," Gumpy said. "She doesn't know anything. She's just hoping that the murderer reads this, and what—gets spooked and makes a move, exposes himself? No, I'm afraid our Sharonda's just ranting, venting some anger. If she knew, she'd be telling us, her father, the detective…"

"Don't you think we should at least call that detective?" This time, James agreed. "Where's his card?"

During Daniel's dinner, about seven–thirty that evening, the phone rang. "Yes, Detective," Daniel said, "I can be there on Saturday morning. Eleven? Sure. And sure, I'll bring the girls; the folks have the weekend off."

Chapter Sixteen:
Sharonda and Connie, just us girls

Lilly didn't care, or notice, but Sharonda didn't like getting up before noon on Saturday, and she voiced her protest. "If you had just told me," she said.

"Then you would have...?" Daniel passed the milk to her, and she poured it on her Cheerios.

She looked at the ceiling for an answer. Finding none there, she said, "Then I maybe wouldn't have talked on the phone all night?" Daniel cracked a smile. So did the fifteen–year–old.

Lilly had nothing to add, except for grabbing at her father's toast and coming away with a little fistful of smashed buttery crumbs. Thus breakfast went smoothly.

Sharonda brought her English book and Lilly slept, so Daniel drove to Indiana in peace. Traffic was light, as it should be on a Saturday morning, but Chicago–area traffic could throw unannounced fits at any time, so he was grateful that all he had to do was dodge groggy sedan drivers and truckers that wanted to be home.

Connie saw them park and opened the door. "Thank you, uh, Connie," Estes said, as his trio all walked into the little lobby. "Didn't expect to see you here on another Saturday."

"It's rare," she said, "except when you're coming, I guess. You're just so special," she bent

way down and said to Lilly," that I've got to make
sure I'm here whenever you visit." Lilly giggled.

Sharonda rolled her eyes and shuffled in place,
anxious to get back to her English book or at least
to sit down and think about something… else.

This morning, Detective Redding came out to
greet them. "I'm Detective Redding," he said.
"Detective Stumpf is already in the interrogation
room."

"I remember you, Detective," Estes said, and
they all started to follow him down the hall.

"Just you, for now," Redding said. Then he
asked Sharonda, "Can you take care of your little
sister for a while, while we old people talk?
Connie can get you some soft drinks, water…"

Sharonda wasn't thrilled, but Lilly had been
quiet and self–absorbed all morning, so maybe
it'd be okay. She wanted to get this stupid book
read, that's all.

Connie said, "I can get you a Pepsi or something,
water for your sister. Want anything?" Then she
looked down the hall, where she saw Stumpf
follow Redding and Estes into the lunchroom.

"Okay, they're gone. Do you want some candy?"
And she pulled a basket of trick–or–treat sized
Snickers, Milky Ways, and Three Musketeers out
of her bottom desk drawer. "Hungry?"

Lilly dove for the basket, but Sharonda stepped
in. "I'll get it for you, Lilly," she said. "Which one
do you like?"

"Clowns," she said, reaching for the Three Musketeers.

"I'll get it for you. You're too little to reach so far." She handed it to the little girl but didn't unwrap it. Looking at Connie, she said, "That'll give her something to do for a while," and giggled.

"How do you know how to handle her so well?" Connie asked. "You're just a freshman, right? But you're so grown up for your age."

Sharonda smiled. "I'm going to be a junior. I guess I'm going to have to grow up faster now. I think I'm going to be the momma around the house now. I'm…" and she stopped talking, put her head down.

"You okay, Sharonda? I mean, here's a tissue. Take your time. Crying helps, you know." She kept going, soothing the teen. "You're awfully young to be in the position you're in. You have all the responsibility of all the kids who start high school; your body is becoming a woman's, boys are way behind you but you can't hang with the seniors."

She looked up. "Yeah, Dad would kill him, if I brought home a senior. Anybody who can drive is too old, he already told me." She looked up. "I don't know if I can do this," she said, and started crying for real, but she was interrupted almost immediately by Lilly, who had gotten her candy bar package open. The bar fell out and hit the floor. Lilly hopped down from her chair, quick as that, and landed on it, slipping and falling, sitting on the smooshed nougat and chocolate.

Connie picked Lilly up and Sharonda grabbed another tissue from Connie's desk, wiped off her little sister's butt. Then, as Sharonda held Lilly still, Connie pulled up a plastic chair and sat Lilly in it, and Sharonda wiped off her shoe, then the floor. Connie said, "There's days like this, I wish we had a dog at the station." She smiled. "You know, for those little messes."

"Chocolate isn't good for dogs," Sharonda said.

"You sound like you have a dog," Connie said. "Boy or girl? Name?"

"He's a boy. He's fixed, though. He's a rescue."

"What's his name?"

"Augie," Sharonda said.

"Strange name for a dog. Well, unusual, anyway." Connie was keeping the conversation going, taking Sharonda's mind off serious things, building rapport, trust, taking care of Lilly together, working as a team without giving or receiving orders.

"Lilly named him, actually," Sharonda said. "We got him like, a year and a half ago, and Lilly wasn't good at saying, 'doggie.' It came out, 'Augie,' so that's what we call him."

Connie laughed, handed her the box of tissues, and excused herself; she returned in a moment with a wet washcloth, and they repeated the process of cleaning up the little girl.

Lilly was again presentable, but seated in the hard chair, she started to cry, and Connie handed Sharonda another Three Musketeers. "Try this one," she said to Lilly. "It's better." And Lilly smiled.

Sharonda sat Lilly far back in the chair and let her attack the second candy bar, which she opened quickly and put in her mouth. "Now, just suck on it," she said, "to get all the flavor." Meaning she wanted Lilly to make this one last a while.

"Thanks, uh…"

"You can call me Connie," she said.

"Everybody around here does, always did. I bet half the people who work here don't know my last name."

"What is it?"

"It's a secret," Connie said, and they both laughed.

Sharonda was relaxing, neither noticing nor caring how much chocolate Lilly was smearing on her face in the vicinity of her mouth. Lilly toddled away down the hall, where Daniel was squatting in the doorway, holding out his arms to the little girl. She got serious. "Do you like working here?" she asked Connie, who nodded. Then, "Why?"

"I started here the summer after I graduated," she said. "My uncle was a lieutenant, a big shot. This city used to be a lot bigger; we had way more people on the force. Anyway, he got me a summer job here in this very station, cleaning up, answering phones, fetching forms, just generally doing whatever needed doing. 'Be nice to people,' he said, 'and be loyal, and you can become anything you want in this world.' That was good advice."

"If you can become anything," Sharonda asked, innocently, "why did you become… this?"

Connie offered her another candy bar. Snickers, this time. "I tell you the truth," she said. "He told me I could do anything, and believe me, I've done everything."

"Did you ever shoot anybody?" Right to the chase.

"No, but I wanted to."

"Really? Who?"

"Somebody different," Connie said. "Somebody different, every day. Sometimes one of the bad guys; sometimes one of my own boys here." She laughed. "But I never had to. Never even saw anybody get shot. Pictures of them, though." She made a face. "Yuk. It's messy!"

Sharonda sat, wide–eyed. "Did you ever catch a crook?"

"Yes, I did. I have this button at my desk that locks the doors there. It looks like a regular little two—door entrance, you know, to keep the cold out, but all that glass? That's all bulletproof. It's really strong. So, if I push this button, it's to let people in, or it locks the doors—all of them. Then the bad guy is stuck in there, like a fish in a fishbowl."

"What if he has a gun?"

"Like I said, it's bulletproof. One time, about ten years ago, this guy had this big handgun, he shot at the glass over there. It got all cracked, but it didn't break. And he shot and shot until his gun was empty. Then when I opened the door and they arrested him, he couldn't hear a thing for two days!"

"That's so cool, Connie!" Sharonda looked at the older lady like she was a superhero. "Can you lock me in?"

Connie said, "Now, you know, different people have different reactions. Some people think it's cool, until they're in there, and they can't get out. They get—like when you're on an elevator and it gets stuck. Did that ever happen to you?"

"Once, in Chicago, when I was real little. But I was with my mom, so I wasn't scared. Can we just try it, please?"

Connie looked down the hall. All was quiet. "Go ahead," and Sharonda bolted for the door. "Okay," she said, when she was between the doors, and Connie pressed the button.

"Try it," Connie said. Sharonda was locked in there, all right. She tried both doors. Connie walked to the inside door and asked through the glass, "How do you feel?"

Sharonda said. "It's okay, but it's kinda creepy. Can I come in, now?"

Connie was walking back to her desk when she heard a yell from the office area. "Connie, come here, quick!" and she ran back down the hall to the break/interrogation room, where Lilly, who had immediately fallen asleep, had slumped off her daddy's lap and hit the floor. She wasn't moving.

Connie pushed the men aside and blew on the little girl's forehead and Lilly opened her eyes. She reached up to Connie, who picked her up as if she were an infant. Lilly smiled and laughed. "I fall down?" she asked, and laughed again.

The men relaxed and Connie handed Lilly back to Daniel, who sat her on the table facing him. "I fall down!" she said, and clapped, laughed again. And all the adults laughed, too.

Connie heard a tapping on the glass out front, where Sharonda was still locked in the fishbowl. Connie hit the switch, and a sweating, heavy–breathing, and upset Sharonda burst into the room. "Why did you do that?" she asked, panting. "I could have *died* in there."

Connie explained what happened and then she calmed down, had another mini-Snickers bar. Then she laughed. "I didn't realize how it feels to just be, you know, locked up like that," she said. Is that what it's like to be in jail?" She was still breathing heavily.

Connie said, "I can't say; I've never been in jail myself." She watched the twinkle return to Sharonda's eyes, and said, "But I have never seen anybody who liked it. You had enough for now?"

"For forever," Sharonda said, letting out a big sigh. "That was really creepy, even though I knew you were coming back. It's not like getting sent to my room at all. It's totally different. Thanks for letting me out."

Connie laughed. "You're the one who wanted to see what it was like, Shar–Shar," and Sharonda got a look on her face that was a mix of disbelief, surprise, and—maybe—terror.

"Shar–Shar? Why did you call me that?"

"I don't know. I just made it up on the spot, kind of like a pet name. Are you okay with that? Did I say something wrong?"

Sharonda swallowed. "No. I mean, it's fine. I just, I never heard anybody call me that before. I didn't know what you were saying, actually."

Connie confessed. "It's your screen name, isn't it?"

"Sharonda dot Estes at funkmail is my screen name, and Sharonda Estes is my Facebook name. Not Shar–Shar."

Connie had already let the cat out. "But Shar–Shar is your other Facebook identity, friends–only. Your dad doesn't know about that one, does he?" Sharonda didn't answer. "Sharonda, we know. We know everything. But your dad doesn't know about Shar–Shar."

Sharonda started to cry. "That's private," she said. "Nobody is supposed to know about that. Just my best, best friends. And now you know. Everybody knows."

"No, honey, not everybody. I know, but I'm your friend, right?"

"Well, yes," she sobbed. "But the detectives?"

"They know, too. And if it has to come out, so will your dad eventually, and his lawyer, and…"

"And the whole world!" Sharonda burst into tears.

"But for now, it's just you and me and your other friends, all right?"

Sharonda kept sobbing. "Did you see… everything?"

Connie put her hand on the girl's knee. "Yes, I suppose so."

"Then you think I'm an awful person."

"No, honey, I don't. I've known some awful people, and believe me, you're not one of them."

Sharonda sniffed, smiled, almost laughed.

Connie continued, "I think you're a normal girl who has been through a lot lately, and you don't know whom to trust. You're scared of the police. You're scared of people you don't even know, bad people who knew your mom. You're even scared of your dad. But don't be scared of me. I'm just an old lady who sees a young lady who's hurting."

Sharonda looked up, eyes teary and bloodshot but grateful. Connie cradled Sharonda's cheeks in her hands, looked into her eyes. "I'm just an old lady… who wants to make a young lady not hurt so much."

"Thanks," Sharonda said. She looked up as her dad, carrying a sleeping Lilly, and the detectives came out front.

"Let's go get some Mickey D's, and go home and have fun," Daniel said to her, and they made their hasty good–byes and trundled into the car.

As they left the parking lot, Daniel asked Sharonda, "What did you and that lady talk about, all that time?"

"She locked me up," Sharonda said. "Can I sleep?" And she leaned against the passenger door and nodded off, her father's repeated questions notwithstanding. Sharonda was disturbed that she hadn't gotten to play Miss Perfect Manners with that fun detective.

Chapter Seventeen: The brief debrief

As Detectives Fred Stumpf and Jerry Redding watched the Estes family pull out of the lot, Stumpf turned to Connie. "Well, what did you find out?"

"She knows we know about 'Shar–Shar,' but we're not going to tell her dad unless it becomes necessary."

"What about that thing about how she knew the murderer?"

"We didn't talk about that," Connie said. "She's a girl. She's scared. She's more scared about our telling her dad about that secret account than she is about anything. We never got around to that."

Redding said, "Then what did you girls talk about for all that time?"

Connie hardened. "I gained her trust. I locked her up." She nodded to the fishbowl. "We talked about Lilly a little. It really didn't come up."

"It didn't come up?" Redding was calm on the outside, raging on the inside. "How did it not come up?"

"Well, Jerry, I didn't see a good time to ask. She's really shook, and she needs a friend. I didn't want to give her any doubts about trusting me."

"Connie," Stumpf said, "I know you have that psychology degree and all, but, cripes, Connie. That's why we dragged the whole family in here, and you got us nothing."

"Fred, Jerry? Can I go home now? It's Saturday, you know, and I'm not on the clock."

"We'll make it right for you, Connie," Fred said. "Really appreciate it. Really."

Then Redding added, "But you know we need to find out what she's talking about. If you can't get it next time, we're going to take over, make her sweat."

Connie laughed. "Look at her wrong and she'll break down… and then clam up. Just have a little patience, Jerry. I've got this. She's got a friend now. She'll tell me what she knows, or think she knows, or whatever that 'I know who the murderer is' meant."

"I hope you're right," Jerry said. "And thanks, Connie. Sorry my frustration is showing."

"That's not like you, Jerry, but we're close to a breakthrough, somewhere. I feel it."

"Well, feelings are good, Connie, but let's get this on the record. Please?" Fred smiled, seeing Jerry so close to a meltdown. The look wasn't lost on Redding, who, nevertheless, said nothing.

"Go home, Connie," Stumpf said. Then to Redding, "We'll find your cigarette pirates, just as soon as we find my murderer."

Connie started to laugh, but when Jerry didn't, she stopped. "Have a good rest of the weekend, gentlemen," she said, as she swept out the door.

Back in Stumpf's office, both detectives sat down. Fred started. "So, nothing from little Shar–Shar," he said. "What did you get from Estes?"

"I'd guess, same as you. Nothing suspicious about his timeline. His answers pretty much add up. Just… something bothers me."

"What is it, Jerry?" Fred said, "The fact that he seems more interested in showing us he knows nothing, than showing any interest in who killed his wife?"

"You put it that way. You have a theory?"

"We always look at the spouse first. But he has alibis and no motive that I can see. He's hard–working, reliable, seems to be a good dad, cares about his kids. Okay, so why is he so worried that we might think it's him?"

"He's wanting to make sure we don't think he's the murderer. But we don't, do we?"

"I don't know. Do we? Who else would Sharonda know?"

"Whom else."

"Oh, stuff it, Jerry. Sharonda says she knows who the murderer is. Who else is in her orbit?"

"Or does she know? She could be faking it. She could be, you know, trying to draw him out, playing tough kid and all."

Stumpf paused a moment. "Jerry, she wrote that on her 'secret' page. Her dad doesn't know about that, or at least he doesn't have her official permission to look at it. So, if she thinks he's the killer, that's why she's hiding it from him. Yes?"

"So, she doesn't include him on her secret page, but she's taunting him there. You think one of her friends is tight with her dad, and that her friend might tell him?"

"Jerry, that doesn't make sense, either. We looked at her friends' list. There's nobody on there over seventeen. How would that connect?"

"Then maybe she knows he knows about it already. How do we get her to tell us?"

"We don't. We ask Daniel."

Stumpf said, "And if that doesn't work, we get her BFF Connie to get her to open up."

"Exactly. How about we go home now?"

Chapter Eighteen: A change of scenery

"Hi, Alfetta," Gino said. "Something special going on today? Wednesday, and all?"

"Hi, Gino. No, just getting some paperwork together for the accountant."

"Accountant? I though you and your dad did all that."

"We keep the books. Taxes are too complicated. We need an accountant for that. So, what's on the docket for today? Where's Eli?"

"He called in sick, said he has a fever or something. For today, we have one of the twenties set for an oil change and a going–over. The last driver said something was squeaking in the back. We don't have any dollies—I keep wanting to ask you, can we get one more? These one–ways are killing us."

"I don't know. Maybe after the accountant gets all this stuff. You think we need another one?"

"More people moving out than in," Gino said. "It's just math. Oh—and there's no babies in the nest any more. Okay if I get rid of it?"

"I'll see what I can do about another car dolly; I think you're right. And yes, that nest is more trouble than I ever could have imagined. If there's no babies in there, take it down. Good idea. Thanks."

Gino got the ladder and checked the birds' nest. It looked abandoned; some leaves had collected in it. He pulled it from its perch atop the surveillance camera and let it drop to the gravel below. He blew on the lens to clear some debris, then checked the cable. It was loose. Not half a turn—it was completely unscrewed. Only friction was keeping in the camera. He cleaned the connector with his fingers and screwed it back in.

As he put the ladder away, he saw Vittorio pull into the lot with a man he didn't recognize in the passenger's seat. Vittorio and the other man joined Alfetta in the tiny office, Vittorio bringing in another chair and then closing the door behind them.

All three of them—Vittorio, Alfetta, and the stranger—left for lunch at a quarter past noon, without saying a word to Gino. In fact, only Alfetta had spoken to him all day. Gino cleaned up the customer area and wiped off the counter top, shined up the windows and the always–fingerprint–smudged door, and then decided to mop the floor.

He rolled up the rented rugs and dragged them out front, where he shook them, beat them with his hand, then laid them in the sun. He had been told they smelled better if you did that. Then he looked for the small broom and dustpan, so he could sweep and wash the floor, but he remembered they were in the office—which was locked. So he went to the cash register that Alfetta called a point of sale terminal, and opened the drawer for the key, but it wasn't there.

Gino decided to mop the floor, broom or no, and mopped as best he could. He was pulling the rugs back indoors when Vittorio's car pulled in. "Looking good, Gino," a smile on his face after a lunch that smelled like alcohol. "We gotta make this place look pristine," he said. He looked at Alfetta, who was shaking her head at him, and he continued, "For the customers. They expect this place to look like a new car lot, not some kind of cut–rate vehicular pawn shop, you know."

"Yes, sir," Gino said, recognizing the boss's condition.

The trio went back into the office without saying another word. Gino faced a slow day, perfect for him, since he had to do Eli's work, too. He changed the oil and found a loose shock absorber on the twenty, and did another inspection on the other truck. He vacuumed and washed the three vans, too.

At six, the office door opened and they all came out in a cloud of bad breath and stale body odor. As Alfetta locked the office door and put the key into her purse, she said, "Good night, Gino. Thanks for doing all that extra work today. You can cover until closing, right? Thanks, honey."

Honey? She never called me that before. What the heck are they doing in there, anyway?

Accountant? Can't they just take the stuff to his office? Whatever's going on, I'm not in on it, that's for sure. Gino wanted to check the cameras, particularly since he had removed the nest and found the loose cable, but the office was locked. *I can't even change the surveillance stick. Hope it's got enough time left on it. Hope the camera's working. Screw it... They don't care, I don't care. Tomorrow.* And Gino locked up and went home.

On a hunch, Gino decided to get his resume together. *Everyone's been a little weird since they found that body. Vittorio was at work more than usual. Alfetta—her hours were all over the place, and she had lost maybe ten pounds, started drinking at lunch, locking the office when she wasn't in there. But today was different. Not just the accountant. Nobody saying anything. Locked doors, no key. And 'Honey?'* Gino didn't recognize the accountant, but he started to think he didn't know Vittorio and Alfetta, either.

Gino liked his job, liked the work, liked the customers. Until today, he thought he liked Vittorio and Alfetta, too. He hoped he still liked Eli, when the kid came back. So he lost interest in writing his resume, started looking for other rental centers where he might soon have to look for work.

As happens on line, soon he was clicking on related links. He had been in the business all his adult life; maybe he could wrangle a franchise or get into an ownership position. Or so he thought, until he saw, under 'Business Opportunities,' a franchised business where the owner was retiring.

Blind ad, but the box had a nearby zipcode. Gino took the leap. Old–fashioned ad, old–fashioned technology. He had a typewriter:

```
Dear Box 3M445:
My name is Gino Sabbatini,
and I have managed the U-
Drive-Em...

.

[blah, blah, blah]

.

I hope you can see a way
to allow me to pay for the
business from its proceeds,
over the next several
years. I would like very
much to please talk with
you. I can start two weeks
from whenever we make a
deal. Thank you.
```

When Alfetta came in the next morning, Gino reminded her that the surveillance stick hadn't been changed. Her question surprised him. "Is anything missing? Broken? Any bodies?" He assured her in the negative. "So there's no problem, is there? I'll change it right away."

He was dazed, but agreed. Then she said, "In fact, I'll be in charge of the cameras from now on. I should be paying more attention to the business. It doesn't run itself, you know."

Gino thought, *Yeah, I know. But I didn't think you knew,* but he just smiled and nodded.

Alfetta continued. "I'll be closing each night. We'll be changing your hours, not so many long days for you. Just from open until six on weekdays." He started to say something, but she cut him off. "You'll be on salary. You'll take home as much as you do now, even though you'll get home earlier. Now, once in a while, I'll need you to stay late, or come in on weekends, and you won't get extra for that, but you'll be money ahead in the long run. I guarantee it."

Gino didn't have time to process all that, so he said, "Sure. That's great. Thanks, Alfetta. When does all this start?"

"Today."

"But it's Thursday. Don't you want me to…?"

"No. Today's the day. You'll be going home early today. Enjoy the time. You've done a great job here, Gino. I really mean that. Thank you."

"Uhhh, thank you, too, Alfetta." And he went into the shop.

Alfetta returned to the office and locked the door.

The accountant appeared after lunch. Gino greeted him at the counter. All he said was, "Alfetta?" and Gino motioned to the office door.

The man knocked, Alfetta opened the door, he went in, and the door locked again.

Gino was glad to have a weekend to relax. He slept in on Saturday morning, went to the mall, did his grocery shopping in the afternoon, and then went to Caballo Loco, a Mexican dive with good food and a long bar. He hadn't remembered the place as being so dark, but then he hadn't been there in three years. He wondered if they had deliberately named the place after the Lakota Sioux chief that wiped out General Custer, his men, and all but one of their horses. He settled in and ordered a draught.

He didn't expect to see Detective Stumpf there. "Hi, Gino. Long time, no see. How're you doing?"

"I'm, uh, fine, uh, Detective. I guess."

"What's up? Any more excitement at the store?"

"Well, not like we had. It's weird, though."

"What's weird?"

Gino took a long draw on his beer. He told Stumpf about the promotion, Alfetta's strange behavior, seeing an accountant for the first time in memory, the locked door. He also mentioned the birds' nest and the loose cable, and that he didn't tell Alfetta about it and couldn't check it because he was locked out of the office. And Vittorio was suddenly interested in the business, too.

"What do you make of all that, Gino? Are they selling the business or something?"

Gino was surprised. "Then it might all make sense, wouldn't it? But… why wouldn't they tell me? And why wouldn't Alfetta run it? I mean, she could do it—she has me—it's making money, and I think it's all paid for."

"Just making up what–ifs, Gino," Stumpf said. "You here for dinner, or just drinking?"

"I could eat," Gino said.

"Let's get a table. Maybe you can bring me up to date. Then I'll pay for dinner and I can write it off on the department. You good with that?"

"Thanks. I'll close out the bar tab here, on me." He called for the tabs and they went to a booth.

"Gino," Stumpf began, "assuming they are going to sell the business, why do you suppose they'd do that? You say it's making money. You know that for a fact?"

"Vittorio told me he's had two record years in a row. And Alfetta just, well, just about, agreed to getting a new car dolly. They also fixed up the building. Remember the roof stuff I told you about?"

"But what about security? If they're making money, and they had this big scare, why haven't they upgraded the security system? And, you know, I love birds as much as anybody, but if a bird was jeopardizing my business, I'd either get another camera—what do they cost, a hundred bucks?—or I'd evict the whole fam-damily of 'em."

"I don't know, Detective. I don't… Hey, I just read about a new place opening somewhere around here. They want to set up a franchise, and they're looking for a manager, or what I hope, an owner."

"Where's that?"

"I don't know. It was a blind ad, but with a zip code near here somewhere."

"Have you heard back from them?"

The waiter appeared, put a bowl of salsa and a basket of corn chips on the table. "My name is Julio, and I'll be your waiter tonight. May I take your order, or do you need a few more minutes?" Gino ordered on a hunch, without looking at the menu. "I'll have the chicken chimichanga dinner, please. And water."

Stumpf said, "The same." Then he focused on Gino. "Have they replied?"

"No. I only did this on Thursday night, a week ago. Mail takes a while. They put the ad on line, but they asked to send a letter to reply. What's that about, anyway?"

"Maybe they don't want to rush into new tech," Stumpf said. "Really, though, if they do that, then you won't be able to bother them too much, can't trace their IP address if they're doing it that way. Maybe they just want to sort out the responses manually and have a lot of people look at them. But you haven't heard back?"

"No. I told them I'd like to work out some kind of deal, where I pay them for the business as I earn the money."

"Well, I know you're a good worker, but they don't know you at all, so…"

"So don't get my hopes up, right?"

Dinner arrived. Stumpf said, "I changed my mind. This water's fine, but I'd like a Dos Equis." He glanced at Gino. "Make that two. Thank you." The beers appeared in real time, before either man had taken two bites of food.

"So," Gino said, "do you know who killed that lady?"

"Can't talk about it, but no, we don't. And we don't know who put her in your truck, either. But we do know that there is a connection between the truck, the murder, and the cigarettes." Almost as an afterthought, he said, "You ever figure out who was messing with the miles on the trucks?"

"No. But there's a funny thing about that. Since I told you about it, since the, uh, murder, there haven't been any more adjustments."

Stumpf looked up from his brown rice. "You think that's a coincidence?"

"I hadn't thought about it much at all, tell you the truth," Gino said, "but… how could it be a coincidence?"

"I suppose it could be," Stumpf said, "like Trump and the Cubs winning in the same year.

But I don't think it's very likely. You sure, none? Not one more adjustment?"

"Nope. I've been keeping my eyes open, even have a little book. It's all balanced out, every day, every truck. Not one single time." Gino took a huge bite of the chimi. He smiled, realizing he wasn't finished talking, but he couldn't talk. He chewed a giant chew and gulped. "You don't think it's a coincidence, do you? So, you want to see my book?"

"Not if there's nothing to see. Like I said," Stumpf grinned, "I can't talk about it. But you call me, if you get some ideas, okay? And hey," he said over his shoulder on the way out, "good luck."

They washed down dinner with the last two Equis, and parted ways.

Chapter Nineteen:
The new normal. Or not.

Gumpy and Nana showed up at the Estes house on Monday morning the same time Gino opened the U–Drive–Em. Nine o'clock at the store; eight o'clock not many miles west, across the time zone in Illinois. All three looked forward to a normal week at their new jobs.

The grandparents were quick to establish a routine. After all, they had raised children before. Visiting and watching Lilly was easy for the experienced and well–coordinated couple.

Sharonda quickly found that her usual tricks didn't work with these old people. But she liked them, too. Because they just told her what was expected—treated her like an adult—Sharonda found it, well, easier to do what was expected, with none of the back–and–forth whining and negotiating, defiance and punishment, that had been her life with her parents. She did at least as much to help, but it didn't seem like she was being forced to do it. Doing what was expected was much more peaceful and more efficient, and she had more time, not less, to do what she wanted to.

Sharonda took down her Shar–Shar page and explained to her friends that she had been caught. She didn't announce it on line. She did it the old-fashioned way: she talked to them. She would let them know when the new page was going up, but it would be at least after they solved her mother's murder, and that it could be years before that might happen.

Gino's first day as a manager was refreshing. He ignored the time clock, started all the systems, opened the register and counted the cash, and noticed that the key to the office was back in its usual place.

He finished up front, and when he went into the office, he was surprised to see how neat, organized–looking, and generally empty it looked. He tapped the surveillance screen and when it came to life, he saw that all four cameras, including the one no longer with the birds' nest and loose cable, were working fine. He checked the surveillance stick, and it said MONDAY, just as it should.

As he closed the office door, the front phone rang. "Thank you for calling U–Drive–Em," he said. "This is Gino. How can I help you?"

Eli came in, waved, went to the time clock, then out to the shop.

"Hi, Gino," the familiar voice on the phone said. "Is Alfetta there?"

"No, Vittorio. I got here ten minutes ago. I haven't seen her. Is she coming here early today?"

"No. But if she comes in, will you have her call me please?"

"Sure, Vittorio. Did you try her cell phone? I can call her if you want."

"No, she doesn't answer. It goes straight to voicemail. Nothing important. Just have her call me when she comes in, will you?"

"Sure, Vittorio. Will do. Uh, hey—she's still coming in at six tonight, right?"

"Far as I know. Tell her to call me. Thanks."

Gino hung up. *Alfetta's not due here until six tonight. Why is he looking for her here, now?* But Gino had a store to run, and didn't give the call another thought.

When Sharonda came home that day from summer session, she found her grandparents asleep on the open hide–a–bed, Lilly dreaming between them. The TV was on, and Hoss and Little Joe were arguing in the background over some wide–eyed gorgeous farm girl, the kind that always seemed to show up near the Ponderosa. Sharonda quietly opened the fridge, poured herself a glass of milk, and tiptoed upstairs. *Cool. They're asleep.* She headed for her computer, planning to be online until Daniel got home.

Daniel was surprised to see the three of them there, still sleeping, glued together with sweat, and no trace of Sharonda except an open refrigerator door and her shoes around the corner in the living room. He stepped over Augie and went upstairs, found his daughter basking in the glow of her screen, earbuds in, oblivious to the time or his presence. He gave the light switch a couple flips and she turned around, startled. She pulled out her ear buds and glared at him as if he'd committed a henious sin.

Her father walked up to her and then sat on her bed, a couple feet from the desk. "Sharonda," he said in a low, calm voice, "You're supposed to let Nana and Gumpy know when you get home, so they can leave and beat the traffic. Do you know it's seven o'clock?"

"Sorry," she said as if she meant it. "I was just… Oh, I'm so sorry. But," and she perked up, "at least rush hour's over and they don't have that traffic."

"Nice try, Kiddle," he said. "No phone until Saturday." He put out his hand. She didn't protest as she put the phone in it.

"I'm really sorry. I… forgot."

"You'll remember better next time, I'm sure," he said. "Now go downstairs and apologize. And don't worry—I closed the refrigerator door that you left open."

"Sorry," she said, as she ran down the stairs, finding her grandparents sitting up and Lilly starting to stir. "Sorry, Nana. Sorry, Gumpy. I just… forgot."

They were standing now. Nana gave her a hug. "We'll see you tomorrow, baby," she said. Gumpy just smiled as he put on his shoes and led his wife to the door. He waved as they left.

"I go bathroom," little Lilly said.

Sharonda admired the new vocabulary. "Okay, Lilly. Let's go into the bathroom now and get you all fresh."

The nearly three–year–old, feeling that she had reached adulthood, proclaimed, "I go bathroom *in* bathroom! Tell Daddy."

Daniel was tired but all smiles when Lilly herself told him. He said, "In the car, everybody. Ice cream!"

Sharonda said sheepishly, "Can we have dinner first?"

Without changing tone, he said, "In the car, everybody. Dinner—at a restaurant!"

On the way home from Denny's, Lilly pooped her pants.

Just about that same time, Gino closed the U–Drive–Em, alone, as he also did on Tuesday.

Wednesday morning, the Fourth of July, Vittorio called him on his cell. "Vittorio," Gino said, "It's, …we're closed. I'm sleeping in. Look, Vittorio," Gino said, "I love working with you and Alfetta. I love my job. But it seems that as soon as I got made exempt, well, I feel like I'm being taken advantage of. I hate to say that; I know you're not that way, but…"

"Gino," Vittorio said, "You're right. I'm a little fuzzy, with how that I can't find Alfetta. I don't mean to be taking advantage. I'll come in at noon tomorrow, make it up to you."

"That's great, Mr. Tonelli, but…"

"I'll see you tomorrow, Gino."

On Thursday, Vittorio Tonelli came in at a quarter 'til six, wearing his U–Drive–Em polo shirt, a relic of the 1980s. He smiled at Gino, asked how everything was going, and what was due for maintenance, who was coming in, and to pick up what; was anything late coming in; and did he like the new car dolly?

Everything was running smoothly, Gino assured him, and then he asked, "Vittorio, where's Alfetta? I appreciate you coming in and all, but… where's Alfetta?"

Vittorio faced the all–glass front wall and waved his arm in a great arc. "She's out there, somewhere," he said. I haven't heard from her since Sunday afternoon. Her car is gone. I went in, didn't touch anything, just looked around. It looks like she took some clothes. She left her phone but took her purse. On Monday, she went to the bank, and took out nearly all the cash from the business account; I couldn't find out if her own account had any activity—they don't give that kind of information to dads." He sighed. "Gino, she's flown the coop."

"Did you call the police?"

"I did, but she's an adult, and there doesn't look like any foul play was involved, so…"

"But the U–Drive–Em account—can't they do something about that?"

"It's her business. She can do whatever she wants with it. She's on the account."

Gino looked down, saw a stone that had been tracked in from the parking lot, picked it up. "Vittorio, do you think this could be, you know…"

"Related to the body in the truck? I don't know how, but what else?" He looked at the phone. "You think I should call the detective?"

"If you don't, I will," Gino said. "Alfetta's on the run. That means she's in trouble. That means something serious is going on, something we don't know about."

"Calm down, Gino. I'm dialing." He mumbled, shaking. "For God's sake, man. I'm dialing."

Detective Stumpf was busy, but he took the statement, asked did he have any idea where she might have gone or why, said he would try to get a warrant, look into her personal account; and would Vittorio please keep him up to date with any information. Vittorio said of course he would.

"Jerry," Stumpf shouted, hoping Detective Redding's door was open and he was in there, "I might have something you're going to find interesting."

Redding came into Fred's office, hung up his sport coat, dusted off a chair, and sat down. "Talk to me."

"Jerry, Vittorio Tonelli called. Alfetta flew the coop. She drove off, looks like on Monday. Stopped at the bank and cleaned out the U–Drive–Em account, left her phone, he said it looks like on purpose. She, some clothes, and her Miata are gone, and she hasn't been heard from since."

"Any ideas why, or where she went?"

"Vittorio's a complete blank. Asked if we could see if her personal account is empty, too."

"We tell the judge, what? That her daddy's wondering how much money she had and if she has enough? Long shot. But why is she missing?"

"Jerry, they're your cigarettes. That makes her your missing person."

"And she's friends with your murder victim. That makes us partners again."

Chapter Twenty: Vittorio's daughter

Jerry Redding called U–Drive–Em, said he'd like to talk with Vittorio. At the store, in person. Vittorio said sure.

"Gino," Tonelli said when he hung up, "I know I said you could go home at noon, but I just talked with the detective and he wants to see me, here, about Alfetta. Could I ask you to stay, just until he's gone?" Gino was expressionless. "Please?"

When Redding arrived, he and Vittorio went into the office. Standard interview for a few minutes, then, "Mr. Tonelli, why did she leave? Your own ideas."

"Well, Detective, she mentioned for a while that she'd like a change of scenery. Really adamant about it, more than asking. She was leaving the business whether I liked it or not. I'm looking to sell the place; even ran blind ads. Funny—Gino answered the ad for a manager, wants me to sell it to him, finance it."

"Does he know it's you?"

"No, I don't think so. And I haven't answered him, either. But Alfetta, ever since her friend, you know, was murdered, she hasn't been herself. She's jumpy, screens her calls, doesn't like to be home alone. She hasn't had a boyfriend for… since last year, but she's got one now, I guess. She doesn't like to be alone and she isn't. But last week, she said she wanted to spend more time here, at the store. She said it was to help get the sale in order, but I think she's just afraid to be alone, even during the day."

"Who's this boyfriend? You ever meet him?"

"No, I don't know anything about him."

"He have a name?"

"Alfetta's private. He was new in her life. She didn't want to get me all introduced, asking questions, if it wasn't getting serious."

Redding tapped his pencil on the note pad. "And it wasn't serious?"

"Like I said, she's private."

"Okay, Mr. Tonelli. You said she left her phone, most of her things."

"Right. I don't know why her phone was there, but, yeah, she can't take too much stuff in a Miata."

"Mind if we go see her place? Do you have a key?"

"I have a key, yes. The place is in my name. She lives there, but it's technically my place." He said, "Are we done here?"

"In this office, yes. Let's go see her place."

Vittorio walked out front, where Gino was with a customer. Tonelli turned to Redding. "Let's give this a couple minutes, okay? Let this guy get on his way?" Redding nodded.

The two of them went to the back, where Eli's feet were sticking out from under a truck. He was doing something greasy. Vittorio leaned way over and made eye contact with the young mechanic. "Eli, as soon as you get to a stopping point, could you please come out? I'd like you to meet someone."

Eli was scooching out in a minute, wiping his hands on a shop towel. "This is Detective Redding," Vittorio said, and Eli held out his greasy hand. Redding looked, hesitated, smiled, and signaled a fist bump. Then motioned to the shop rag and Eli handed it to him. Redding wiped his knuckles. "He would like to ask you a couple questions." Vittorio motioned to the break area, asked if anyone wanted a drink. They said yes, and he opened the machine. "Help yourselves," he said, then took out a root beer for himself and locked it back up.

Redding started. "Eli, right? Eli, this murder has us wondering how U–Drive–Em could possibly be connected. We found the lady's body in the truck. Well, you did. I know you've been asked before, but we're not looking for facts. You told us everything already, right?"

"Right, sir. I think about it a lot, and I can't think of anything else, that I didn't tell you already."

"Well, you be sure to call us any time, if you do, okay? Doesn't matter what time it is. You remember something, you tell us." Eli nodded.

Redding continued, "I'm glad you think about it, Eli. Here's the thing: we police aren't coming up with anything that makes sense between Lulita and U–Drive–Em. She never rented here, lived an hour away, but there she is, in your truck. I'm not looking for more facts—unless of course you remember or find some—I'm looking for… What do you think, Eli? What is Lulita Estes's connection to U–Drive–Em?"

Eli looked at Vittorio, and Vittorio nodded. "Tell him whatever you think, Eli. We're all trying to figure this out. You won't get in trouble."

Vittorio looked down at his Mountain Dew.

Redding looked at Vittorio, and Vittorio said, "Tell you what, Eli. I have some stuff to do out front." He looked at Redding. "I'll be in the office or at the counter, whenever you're ready." He looked at Eli with calm eyes. "Take your time, son. Let's get this figured out." Redding waited for Eli to talk. Just waited.

"Well, I," Eli started, then stopped.

"You...?"

"Yeah, I know this sounds maybe crazy, but wasn't Alfetta friends with that lady?"

Redding nodded.

"And Alfetta's gone now, and nobody knows where she's gone?"

Redding nodded again.

"Well, isn't that some kind of connection?"

Redding said, "You mean, more than a coincidence?"

"Yeah. Alfetta's always been here. She's always looking at the paperwork, making a big deal over a spot on the floor, making sure the trucks get maintenance. Then her friend shows up in the truck, and now she's disappeared. That sounds like this is all connected to here somehow."

"Do you know how?"

"I… I don't want to say. If I'm wrong…"

"Eli, we're just playing 'what if?' here. There's no right or wrong. It's just guesses. If you're wrong, nobody gets hurt. But hey, if you're right, maybe you can help solve a murder. Of if Alfetta's in some kind of danger, maybe help her out."

"Okay. Well, sometimes Alfetta would ask me to do weird stuff, like clean out the truck when it was already clean. 'Give it another good sweep,' she'd say. But it was already clean. I'd get, like, half a dustpan more dirt, sweeping the whole truck. Or sometimes she'd say to check a truck to make sure it was going to be roadworthy for a big trip. She'd say, 'for a big trip,' but nobody would even take it out 'til Monday, and she would tell me on Friday, and the trucks are always ready. If they're not, I put the tag on them, and we fix it right away. She's been kinda weird that way, lately."

"Lately?" Redding said. "Lately, like since Christmas?"

"Well, almost. Maybe more like Valentine's Day. But a lot until... until the body."

"Why do you think she's doing that? You think she's got something to hide?"

"No. There's never anything special wrong with the trucks—I fix that, and I make sure they're clean. It's... she's different."

"How, different?"

"Well, right about that time, real cold winter, she put those hand sanitizer things in the front on the counter, and one in the bathroom, and another one in the office. And she uses them all the time. She still does that. Makes the rest of us feel like we've got cooties or something."

"She never did that before?"

"No. She was, you know, normal. She washed her hands in the bathroom, sure, but that's just what you do."

"How do you know?"

"Because she'd open the door, soon as she was finished, you know. And the door would be open, and she'd be washing her hands."

"Does she still do that?"

"Yeah. And then she goes to the counter, or to her office, wherever... and she squirts that hand sanitizer on. And she just washed her hands."

"Anything else weird that you noticed?"

"No. Well, yes, sort of. Gino told me she makes up the mileage, puts down miles on other trips, when one trip did the miles."

"What do you mean? Can you give me an example?"

"No, I don't really know anything about that. You can ask Gino. But don't tell him I told you, okay?"

"Okay, I won't. Anything else?"

"Well, since that body… Since then, she makes me and Gino park the trucks where the camera can see them. We used to just park them, you know, wherever there was room, but now, everything has a special place to park. And she checks."

"Thanks, Eli. Anything else you think of?"

Eli had finished his Mountain Dew. "I think that's all I've got for now, Officer. Can I go back to work now? That truck needs a new driveshaft support bearing, and I'm almost done putting it in. But the customer's coming, I don't know when, but today."

"Sure, Eli. And thanks. And please, if you think of anything, or you get a theory, you call me, okay?"

"I will, sir." Redding turned. "Sir?"

"Yes, Eli?"

"Did you ever figure out who took the license plate off the truck, or why?"

Redding whirled. Eli told the story. "Did Gino tell you to put the plate back on?"

"No. I just figured it was off, so I put it back on. I didn't think about it until just now."

Redding made a note to see if the techs had gotten prints off that plate, either side. "Thanks, Eli."

He met Vittorio out front, where a customer was just leaving, having returned a van. "Ready?" Vittorio asked, and Redding nodded. "Then follow me."

Redding followed the Lincoln to a nice but not ostentatious apartment complex not far from the store, followed Vittorio up the outdoor stairs to Alfetta's landing. Redding thought the building was reminiscent of a motel.

The apartment was orderly, even if it hadn't been vacuumed in a while. Nothing out of place. Refrigerator half empty, but nothing in it was out of date. Vittorio hadn't touched anything when he looked around, he said. He hadn't even touched Alfetta's phone, which was on the kitchen counter, charged and still plugged into the charger.

"She ever pull this before?" Redding asked.

"You mean, disappearing? Not since she was a teenager," Vittorio said, "and she never leaves her phone anywhere. It's not more than a couple feet away. It's in her purse, or she's using it, or she's sleeping and it's on her nightstand."

Redding's mind lurched. "Vittorio, now, very carefully: She charged it on her nightstand, next to her bed?" He nodded. "Then why is it charging on the counter?"

Vittorio looked perplexed. "Because she wanted me to know she left without it? But why?" Redding waited. "If she kept the phone, wouldn't she be easier to track?" Redding stayed silent. "So, she wants us to know she left, and she doesn't want us to know where she is." And again, Redding stayed quiet, letting Vittorio think out loud. "But why would she leave and want us to know she left? Left on her own, but not want us to know where?"

Vittorio's look was sad, helpless, pathetic, a father who just realized something terrible about his daughter. She needed him, but she was afraid to tell him why. And he didn't know how to help her. Vittorio walked over to a sofa. "May I sit down?" Redding nodded. Vittorio collapsed into the couch, a blank look on his usually sharp face, staring at the empty table across the room.

Redding said, "Alfetta's a smart girl. She knows we can find the Miata on an APB, you know, all–points bulletin, or if she sells it somewhere and switches to another car, but that's not easy for a non–law enforcement person to do. Finding out where a lost cell phone is, is actually easier. Or maybe there's a message on the phone, or information—for sure, it will tell us whom she called, and when. I'll take it to the lab. With your permission, of course."

Vittorio nodded. "Of course." And he opened a kitchen cabinet, pulled out a ziplock bag, and handed it to Redding, who loaded the phone into the bag by handling everything as one piece -- phone, cable, charger -- and wrapping the bag around everything.

Vittorio watched, then asked, "What else do you want to see, Detective?"

"How about everything, but first, the bathroom. And can you bring those bags, please?"

Using a bag between his hand and anything else, Jerry Redding went through the cabinets, picking up various items, stopping when he opened a bathroom drawer with some plastic prescription vials in them. He read the labels as he bagged them. All with her name on them, a few he recognized. Antibiotics, antihistamine, cough suppressant—all normal stuff, dated last winter. And new pills, too, with nine refills yet to go, for anxiety. All these went into the bag. He asked Vittorio, "When did she start seeing a shrink?"

Vittorio looked surprised. "I—we always joked that we both needed one, but I didn't know she was seeing anybody for real."

"Well," Redding said, "That's what this Doctor Fu is, a shrink, and she has nine refills left, so he's been seeing her a while—looks like maintenance medicine."

Her father said, "Why would she leave those behind?"

Redding shook his head, bagged the pills. "Bedroom?" Vittorio led the way.

Nothing looked out of place. The bed was made, slippers tucked under the end of the bed, robe hanging on a hook on the outside of the closet door. Inside the closet, a few empty hangers—not too many—and ten pairs of shoes. "How many shoes did she have?" Redding asked.

"I don't know," Vittorio said. "I recognize those, and those… but… But it's weird. She had at least three pairs of gym shoes. There's none here. And her hiking boots are gone, too."

"Let's see her dresser," Redding said. "Did she have a lot of jeans, outdoor clothes?"

"No, just those fancy designer jeans," Vittorio said, "that I remember. She wasn't very outdoors–y." He looked around, on shelves, in the drawers.

"Easy, Vittorio. Let's be methodical about this. Let's just do this together."

"Okay, but, you know, she took her hiking boots and she doesn't hike. She got those when she joined some outdoors club years ago. Went on one outing, hated it. But she kept those boots, just in case, or something. And now she took them, and––you're not finding those jeans, either, are you?"

"Does that all give you an idea where she might have gone?" Redding asked.

"Outdoors, where she can just be, you know, 'free,' and not need her pills. And need her boots and jeans."

"Vittorio, do you remember where she went with the outdoors group?"

"It was… Yeah, I remember, she said the traffic was terrible going through Chicago. Yeah, she went to someplace in Wisconsin, just over the border." Vittorio lit up. "Sounded like a kitchen."

"Kettle Moraine?" Redding asked.

"That's it! Kettle Moraine. Rained all weekend, had a tent–mate she didn't like, hated the traffic. Kettle Moraine. They spent most of the time in the common building, taking turns going to town for beer. You know, Wisconsin." He laughed, nervous. "Yeah, sounded like a kitchen. Close enough, I guess. Kettle Moraine." Then he calmed down, hesitated, about to talk. Then, finally, "You think she went there?"

"Well, you said she's not outdoors–y, and she doesn't want to get found, so why not hide out in the great outdoors? No meds, but she won't have to talk to people. And it's not far away, if she changes her mind." Redding paused a minute. "It's still a long shot, but when you don't have any other shot, what shot do you take?"

Vittorio and Redding both said, "The long shot."

Chapter Twenty–one: The missing Miata

Redding booked the new evidence, asked Artie to find out everything he could from Alfetta's phone, and called down the hall, even as he walked that way. "Connie, can you see if a Mazda Miata, three years old, has just been registered in Illinois or Wisconsin. Just registered, like, since Sunday." He reached her desk. "Here's the VIN," and he handed her a scrap of paper.

"Jerry, it's Thursday." Connie was standing there behind her desk in the lobby, holding the slip of paper. "Okay, what color is it?"

"Silver," he said. "But, yeah, it's a little early, isn't it? What we can do, a lot quicker, is an APB on the car. There's probably a single woman, looks about forty. Alfetta Tonelli has run off somewhere. Her father thinks maybe southern Wisconsin, northern Illinois, along Lake Michigan. Check campsites, too. And run her credit cards, see if she's left a trail. Gas stations, fast food… Oh, and here's her license number."

"And what would you like me to do after lunch?" It was eleven–thirty.

"Just, please, Connie. Okay, start with the APB, then the credit cards, then whatever you think will be fastest." Redding said, "I'm going to see Tree."

"Detective Stumpf is at lunch," Connie said. "In Illinois. At Sharonda Estes's high school. Or at least he's on his way."

Never mind. Don't tell me. I'll call him. You see if you can find that Miata. Thanks, Connie."

Redding hung up his jacket, went into the break room and poured the morning's last cup of coffee from the burned pot, turned off the coffee maker, and went back to his office. He called Detective Stumpf. "Tree? Yeah, we have a thin hope on Alfetta's destination. Connie's on it. Some weird stuff there at the rental place. I'll tell you later. So, why are you headed to have lunch with a fifteen–year–old?" He sipped the coffee.

Redding made a face in response to the awful brew. "Connie? Yeah, I just saw her when I came in. No, you tell me… What? Yeah, I have something, maybe. Maybe nothing. I don't know anything yet, about anything. Okay, and you tell me if you find out anything. Sheesh. Good–bye."

Artie, from the lab, came into Redding's office without knocking. Then he stopped, backed out to the hallway, leaned in and, wearing a silly grin, lightly tapped on the open door.

"Nobody home," Redding said. "Come in, Artie. What do you have? What are you even working on? Don't you go to lunch right about now?"

"Well, I went into that iPhone you gave me, from the lady in the truck."

"Twenty minutes ago?"

"No, the first one. Well, it wasn't damaged, so I went right in."

"Damaged?"

"Yeah. It had water in it. Probably didn't work for a couple days, but it's dried out now, and I was able to get into it."

"What did you find in there, Artie?" Redding was getting hungry. He had skipped breakfast. All he had was a diet soda at the rental place and that gut–ripping coffee. "You want to tell me over lunch? I'll buy." Anything to get some food.

"No, Detective Redding, sir," Artie said. "I can tell you everything in just a minute."

"Spill it, Artie."

"Okay, Detective, I ran the file analysis on the iPhone, and…"

"Artie? Get to it."

"There's nothing on the phone."

"What?"

"It's been reset, erased, wiped. It's like a new phone—there's nothing there but a few apps. Water didn't hurt it, but the SIM card is ruined. Nothing on it, if there ever was."

"So, the phone tells us…?"

"Nothing at all, Detective. But there's prints on it. I've got good prints at least. I don't know whose they are, yet."

"Thanks, Artie." Redding slumped into his chair. He never slumped, but he felt this was an occasion to slump, so he took advantage of the moment. "So, lunch?"

"Thanks, Detective, but I've still got a couple things I have to do." Artie didn't want to be Redding's company when Redding was going to be such lousy company.

Redding called Stumpf and told him about Lulita's secret and useless phone, as he drove to lunch.

* * *

Stumpf pulled into the Thornridge High School lot, stopped at the metal detector and explained his business, showed his badge, and waited while the lady at the door called the principal. "Of course, Detective," she said. "Just wait here, and Sharonda's counselor will be with us in a moment."

"I'm here for Sharonda, not her counselor," Stumpf said. "She knows that, right?"

Miss Tweedlesnit, the counselor, appeared from around the corner. "Hello," she said. "I am Sharonda's counselor, and I'm afraid our school policy does not allow anyone to interview our students without their parents' permission." That wasn't her name, but it's the name that popped into Stumpf's head, the moment he saw her.

Lorraine Davenport, her real name, was about five–feet and no inches tall, and carried her hundred and eighty pounds mostly and ungraciously below her waist. Her shoes made an annoying clacking sound as she approached, but

Stumpf was certain he'd enjoy the sound they'd make, leaving.

Stumpf said, "She wants to talk with me. Alone. She called me, said she didn't want her father present. Now, I don't know about your policy, but this is a murder investigation. The murder of one of your colleagues, in fact."

"I'm sorry, officer," she began.

"Detective."

"I'm sorry, *Dee–tec–tive,* but we have our policies. Furthermore, I see you are from Indiana, and I don't need to remind you that we are in Illinois. So I must ask you to please leave our school grounds, immediately."

Stumpf didn't move. He said, "I'm not here to be difficult. I just drove half the afternoon because a sophomore here, who has just lost her mother, your librarian, called me and said she wanted to talk to me about her mother's murder. Surely there's something in your policies that would allow us to talk."

"You must leave, now," Davenport said.

"Or, what? You'll call the police? Look, this is a police matter, and you're interfering with a police investigation." He left.

Back in his car, Stumpf called the office. "Hi, Connie. Yeah. Do you perhaps know any judges in Cook county? Maybe a prosecutor here, if you don't. I need to get a warrant to go into this school where Sharonda is. Yeah, by three o'clock…

Yeah, I know it's two–fifteen. I need it by three… Yeah, go ahead…" And he wrote down the phone number and address. "Connie, you are unbelievable! Yes, of course I love you. Everybody loves you."

Stumpf got to the courthouse in five minutes, up the stairs to room 304, and into Judge Cofeve's office, where he announced himself. The secretary told him he was expected and handed him some papers, already partially filled out.

"Wait out here," she said. "Fill these out the rest of the way, and I'll tell the judge you're here."

Judge Linda Cofeve looked like Connie's twin, so similar that Stumpf did a double–take as she extended her hand to shake. But no taupe beret. "So," as she reviewed the paperwork, "the school wouldn't let you in without a warrant? Why don't you just interview this girl at her home?"

"It's in there, your Honor," he said. "Sharonda said she couldn't talk with other people around. She's scared."

"Of what? Of whom?"

"She didn't say. Her grandparents are there when she gets home; I don't think she's afraid of them, but they would certainly tell her father I was there…"

"She's afraid of her father?"

"That's what I'm trying to find out, your Honor."

She took the papers and signed two sets. "Well," she said, "you'd better hurry. Good luck."

"Thank you, judge," and he was out the door and back to the high school.

It was twenty minutes before three.

"Back so soon?" said the lady at the metal detector, as Stumpf handed her the warrant.

"Yes, it's a good day in the neighborhood. Go, Falcons!" he said, as he took back the papers and went to the office, whence an irritated counselor Lorraine Davenport shortly appeared with Sharonda.

"Do you need privacy?" she asked.

"Ma'am, this is a police matter. Yes, we do. Maybe you have a room with some glass, so you can watch us, if that's what your concern is."

"We don't let our students meet with adults unless their parents are present, or, if this is about her mother's murder, without their lawyers," she said.

"You're going to make an exception this time, though," he said, "unless you want a whole SWAT team in here, all day tomorrow." Bluffing, but convincing.

Davenport nodded, led Sharonda and Detective Stumpf to a glass–walled conference room, left them, and shut the door.

Sharonda smiled. "Thank you for coming to see me," she said. "I wanted to talk to… that lady at the station, but I really wanted to talk to you, but I didn't get a chance, and my dad was there, and..."

And she looked like she was about to cry. She fumbled around in her backpack and produced some tissues, wiped her cheek.

"Well, it's okay now," Stumpf said, in as calming a voice as he could muster. "We don't have much time, though, and I know you called about something important." He smiled a bit and said, "So, what's on your mind, Sharonda?"

"Remember that post I made, where I said I knew who killed my mom? Well, I don't really know."

Stumpf hid the frustration, even the anger inside. He had been nursing an ulcer for months, and he felt that it was about to open wide up.

Sharonda said, "But I know that there's a lot weird that happened that night." Stumpf's expression didn't change. She continued. "Mom was home that night, late. I heard her talking with Dad."

Stumpf said, "The night she... was killed? You're sure? Maybe you were dreaming. What time would you say it was, when you think you heard them? What were they saying?"

Sharonda stumbled a bit, wiped her eyes again. "It was around twelve–thirty, maybe one o'clock. Maybe later, a little. I was up late, reading. I think I put the book away at—I get in trouble if I'm up past midnight, even if it's studying. So I think it was maybe a couple minutes before midnight when I turned the light off, but I wasn't totally asleep and I heard them talking."

"What were they talking about?"

"I—I don't know. I just heard them talking. Then I went to sleep."

"You're sure you heard them, not just some 'I'm almost asleep and I'm half–dreaming' kind of thing?"

"I'm positive," she said.

"And you're positive about the time?"

"Not totally positive," she said, "but I'm sure it wasn't, like, right when I turned out the light, or real, real late, like three or four."

Stumpf pressed on. "Did you get up, check to see? Did you look at the clock, maybe, or look out the window, see if the cars were there?"

"No," she said. "I just went to sleep. Woke up when they called about Mom."

"So, let me get this straight: you are sure, you're positive that you heard your parents talking that night, some time after midnight, but probably not, as you say, super, super late. And you don't know what they were saying." She nodded. "What was their tone of voice? Were they fighting, just talking, or what?"

"Sounded like they were just talking," she said. "Kinda shout–whispering, if you know what I mean. Not their real, you know, daytime voices.

But they didn't sound mad or anything. I think I heard Mom laugh maybe a little."

"Anything else you remember, Sharonda? We're going to have to wrap this up." She shook her head. "And you don't tell *any*body what we talked about, you hear? Especially not those busybodies on the other side of the glass."

She looked through the window at Davenport and one of the teachers, not one of her teachers. "What should I tell them?"

"Just tell them I had a couple questions, and you didn't know the answers, and… that's it. What those questions were, that's police business and you can't talk about it. Got it?"

"Yes," she sniffed. "That makes sense. And thank you so much, Officer."

"Detective."

"Oh, yes, sorry. Detective." She zipped up her bookbag. "I've gotta go now. Thanks again."

"Thank you, Sharonda. "Remember, if you think of anything, anything at all, call me."

"I will. Thanks. 'Bye."

Stumpf was stopped in traffic on the Interstate, just shy of the Indiana border. It was ten minutes of four—almost five for Connie, who was ringing his phone. "Stumpf," he answered.

"Hi, Fred," Connie's friendly voice came through like a cool shower in the desert.

"You know that Miata you had me look for, that would be impossible to find, since it's been gone with Alfetta Tonelli for just, like, a couple days or so?"

"Connie, don't tell me you found it."

"No, I didn't. A sheriff near Lake Geneva, Wisconsin found it. Two kids in it, a boy, twenty, and a girl, same age. He drove it off the road into a ditch and his buddies tried to tow him out, and they flipped the car over. The kids are okay, but the boy's in jail. Blew a point oh–nine. Jerry's on his way there now."

Stumpf said, "So, how did you find it so fast?"

"It still had Alfetta's plates on it. The boy had the title, too, signed by it looks like Alfetta. Said she traded him straight up for his car on Sunday night, at some dive between Racine and Kenosha."

"Okay, Connie. What car are we looking for now? And did Alfetta keep his plates on it?"

Connie laughed. "Looks like our Alfetta was in a hurry to trade. She traded her Miata for a 2005 PT Cruiser. The boy said he went home and got the title and forged his mom's name on it. He said he didn't take the plates off when he traded; he wanted to get out of there before she changed her mind. I've got the plate, and I've already called Madison, gave the State Police all the info. Wisconsin's issuing an APB for a red PT Cruiser with a bad negotiator in it. I already told Jerry. If they find her, they'll hold her on the phony plates and title sig. Jerry'll pick her up for..."

Stumpf interrupted. "Connie, you are the best."

"I know, Fred. So I'm getting a raise?"

"Not my department, doll, but you know I'll bring you a thank–you card if I ever think of it."

"Drive safe, Fred. Jerry's got this. Come home. Connie out here."

"You're the greatest," he said, but the call was over.

Chapter Twenty–two: A short PT cruise

Friday morning, after a relaxing day walking the woods and looking at the small lakes of southern Wisconsin, Alfetta was cursing her trading the Miata for the PT Cruiser when she was stopped for running a yellow light, heading south on US 41, just inside Illinois. She apologized for the plates and showed the new title, explained how she was excited to get home to Indiana with her new car, flashed straight white teeth, and got off with a warning. It was a lucky stop for her; local police rather than state. He didn't call it in. And Illinois hadn't gotten the APB from Wisconsin. Alfetta continued south, toward Chicago. Fifteen minutes later, the APB came over the local cop's radio.

North Chicago PD called State and County, told them the Cruiser had been going south, probably headed for Indiana. Alfetta, without any particular destination in mind and in no particular hurry to get there, was relaxing at a roadside Burger King when the trooper came in.

As the flatbed took her PT Cruiser away, Alfetta and the trooper filled out paperwork over coffee in the corner of the restaurant, far from the door. Illinois didn't want Alfetta any more than they wanted to store the car, and the Illinois State Police were happy to wait for Jerry Redding, who arrived in half an hour, from the north.

"Sorry it took so long," he said, "and thank you for holding on to my suspect," He turned to Alfetta. "Nice to see you again, Miss Tonelli. Are you ready to go back to Indiana?"

"Nice to see you, Detective. But... how did you get here so fast?"

As she stood up and Redding cuffed her behind her back, he said, "It's a cop secret, but I was coming home from where a couple kids wrecked your Miata."

They filled out some paperwork for the trooper, walked her out to Redding's car, and opened the back door. "Watch your head," he said, as she slid in. He buckled her seat belt, went around front, and slid into the driver's seat for the long ride home.

"Glad the Sox aren't playing today," he said as they passed 31st Street, where Comiskey Park once stood; he hated the new corporate naming that the leagues were all getting into. "Or Chicago traffic'd be even worse." And they didn't say anything to each other, all the way back to Indiana.

After they Mirandized Alfetta and booked her into the jail, Vittorio Tonelli arrived, demanding that his daughter be released. "Sorry; the judge doesn't work this sort of case 'til Monday," was the only answer he got. Tonelli left a message for his family lawyer.

He had never used her for anything, but she was cute and was on retainer. He didn't ask, and she didn't volunteer what kind of legal work she did, or even if she did any criminal work.

Alfetta skipped dinner and made herself as comfortable as she could. And waited for Monday morning.

Bright and early, well, early on Monday morning, Heather Geyer asked to see her new client, and she introduced herself to a hungry, grouchy, and disheveled Alfetta. "Just work with me here," she said, "and you'll be having breakfast with your father shortly. He's waiting, and the judge will be setting your bail any minute now."

"What am I charged with?" Alfetta asked. Geyer chuckled. "Driving a car that wasn't yours," she said. "In Illinois." You'll be out of here as soon as the judge sits down at her bench. I've got to go now. You're either first, or nearly first. Be good, don't say anything to anybody, and you'll be out of here as soon as court opens up." Alfetta nodded.

Half an hour later, Vittorio and Geyer were back. "Are you hungry?" Vittorio asked.

"Oh, Daddy," she said. "Let's just go home."

Redding and Stumpf were almost playing hookey, having late breakfast at Aunt Tatter's, "Famous for pancakes, rolls, and other good stuff." Not true hookey, though—they were talking business, and how the cigarettes, Alfetta, and Lulita were all related.

Every seat at the counter was full when she walked in, except the one stool on the end, next to Stumpf. "May I?" she asked him, and he nodded.

Then, unexpectedly, she introduced herself, maybe because the three of them were dressed for business. "Heather Geyer," she said. She looked around at the rest of the place, nervous as all the flannel shirts and t–shirts and tattoos turned her way.

She was a striking lady, just shy of thirty, maybe just over. Expensive bottle-blonde hair, navy blue suit, shiny pumps, designer handbag. "I'm a lawyer," she said. "I usually do wills and trusts, but today I was getting a client out of jail, this morning, I mean. " She made a point of looking at his shirt, where a blind lady could have seen the vest underneath. *Obviously a cop. White shirt. Probably detective.* "You know Alfetta Tonelli?"

Stumpf looked at Redding, who shrugged his shoulders as if to say, "She's talking to you. Don't get me into this."

Stumpf, wondering why she felt obligated to explain her presence but noticing that she was a beauty, even if she was a little crazy or something, said, "I'm Fred Stumpf. I'm a detective. I work just around the corner. Nice to meet you."

"A detective?" she said, "Do you know another detective, a fellow by the name of Redding?"

Redding kicked him. Stumpf said, "Yes, we work together now and then. Why do you ask?"

Geyer went into a long description of how she had heard a lot about Jerry Redding, how he was a legend among certain people in town, and how he was supposed to be so smart, and how he was the one who had locked up her client.

Stumpf just listened as she said she had done her research on him, how he was past his prime probably—don't you agree?—and how she was ready for anything.

Then, just as abruptly, she stopped and apologized. "I'm way out of line. I'm so sorry. I didn't mean to say that. I mean, he must be a friend of yours." She took a gulp of her coffee, left a ten–dollar bill on the counter for the breakfast that hadn't yet arrived, excused herself, and hurried out.

Stumpf looked at Redding. "What the hell was that?" he said. Again, Redding just shrugged. "And why didn't you tell her who you were?"

"Why?" Redding answered. "She already knows all about me."

Her meal arrived, and Stumpf pushed his empty plate aside, motioned to the now–empty spot in front of himself, and said to the waitress who looked at the empty place where Heather Geyer had been when she ordered, "You can leave that here. Thanks."

Redding shook his head and pulled out his little book as Stumpf swallowed Geyer's breakfast.

"Fred, Lulita and Alfetta were up to something together here, that's pretty obvious. Lulita used Alfetta's trucks, and Alfetta covered for her. I don't think Vittorio knows anything about what's going on."

"You think Gino does?"

"He's suspicious about whatever Alfetta's doing to the mileage reports, but he stays away from the paperwork end of the business. I think he's more into the customers and the trucks. No, I don't think he knows. I don't think he's involved. But he knows something is going on."

"So, do you think he'd be any good as a witness?"

"To what? I mean, he already told us the mileage gets fiddled with; he'd be good as far as that goes. But he didn't even know about the birds' nest. Just thought the camera was going on the fritz lately."

"But he also didn't change the USB stick," Fred said. "Why?"

"Maybe because he forgot. Or maybe he did, and Alfetta switched it out for a different one. But the camera wasn't showing any more than the one side of the truck, anyway. You couldn't see around the back, just along that one side."

"Yeah, and Gino knew that, too, didn't he? And Gino parked that van, or had that kid, Eli, do it. At the very edge of the camera's vision."

"Also in the last open slot on the lot," Redding said. "Must have parked the car off the end of the building. Coincidence?"

Stumpf continued to look straight at him. So Redding said, "Chicken or egg, you're saying?"

"Right. Did he park it there because it was the only open slot, or was that the only slot precisely because it was the only space that didn't have decent coverage?"

"Or was it luck, or some system they have?" Redding said. "Or was the system designed to put a big truck in a blind spot?"

"To U–Drive–Em?" Stumpf asked, having put away his second breakfast. "Shall we?"

"To U–Drive–Em," Redding replied, picking up both checks and heading to the register.

"Thanks," said Fred.

Redding looked back over his shoulder. "Tip," he said, and Stumpf pulled out a five and three ones, put them on the counter.

"Thanks for breakfast," Stumpf said, as they got into the car. Then, "Wait a minute. I just left a cash tip, and you got the receipt. You're going to get reimbursed, and I…"

"You just left a cash tip, but you also got two free breakfasts. Stop whining and wipe the egg off the corner of your mouth." Redding smiled, started the car, and they headed to see Gino.

Gino smiled as the two detectives came in. Not because he was particularly glad to see them. More a smile of recognition, the kind of smile he gave regular customers. Customers who weren't investigating smuggling and murder, anyway. "Good morning, Detectives."

"Gino," Stumpf said, "we need to talk." He nodded toward the break area.

Gino said, "I'm here alone for now. Can we just talk here?" Stumpf nodded, still standing on the customer side of the counter.

"Gino, we're at a couple dead ends. We know Alfetta and her deceased friend used your trucks to take loads of cigarettes into Illinois, so that's a crime. A big, fat federal crime. But worse, we have a murder. The victim was in your truck. We don't know if she was killed here or somewhere else, but we know she drove that truck on the night she died."

Gino nodded, wondering where this was going.

"And the truck," Redding tool over, "your truck, was parked in the only spot on the lot that the camera doesn't cover. Do you find that curious? We kind of do. Tell us all about why that particular truck was parked in that particular spot."

Gino had his question, but no idea of how to answer it. "It—it just always got parked there," he said. "Each thing, each kind of thing—big trucks, little trucks, dollies, vans—each is always parked in the same area. I mean, either twenty–footer could be in either spot for a big truck, but we'd never park a van there, just like we'd never park a big truck in a van spot." He looked at Redding, then Stumpf. "Is that what you mean?"

Without acknowledging or answering his question, Redding continued, "Maybe I'm a little late asking, but who set up the cameras?"

"I did," Gino said. "We got them three, maybe four years ago."

"How did you decide to place them, or did somebody tell you where?"

"Uh, Vittorio, he told me he wanted one here, one for the shop, outside back, front."

"Did he tell you what to cover?"

"No, not really. I just moved the cameras around—he was watching from inside; we were on our cell phones. He'd say, 'That's good,' and I'd clamp it down. Then, when we had a storm or something, you know, if a camera got moved, I'd just put it back to show what it showed before."

"Are those all the original cameras?"

"Yes." Gino hesitated. "Well, no. We had one go bad, the one here in the customer area. We replaced it last year. But it was the same camera, same model. Just a new one."

Stumpf asked the next question. "So, getting back to the camera where you cleared the bird's nest: when you parked the big trucks, you know that the camera only covered the passenger side and not the back?"

"Sure. It was always that way."

"Was there ever a time when both trucks might be out at the same time, and they could switch places when they came back? You have only two spaces for big trucks, right?"

"Right. And sure, there are lots of times when they're both out, or one's out and one's in maintenance. When they come back, just whatever spot is open. It doesn't matter which one goes where. We just put 'em…"

"Okay," Stumpf interrupted. "Got it. Let me ask you something else. Alfetta."

"What about Alfetta?"

"Do you and Alfetta…?"

"What?" Gino leaned back, smiled stupidly. "Me and Alfetta? Wow. No way. She's the boss's daughter. She's my boss. And besides, she's, you know, old. No. Never. No way."

"Okay, just wondering. Did she ever talk about her personal life, maybe somebody named Tony?"

Gino thought for a moment. "Tony… First, she never talked about her personal life, and second, we're hardly ever here together at the same time. Tony… ummm, I don't know if it's important; I don't think he's a boyfriend or anything, but, yes, I remember a call a few weeks ago. He said he was Tony, would I please get Alfetta on the line."

"What did you do?"

"I went and told Alfetta a guy named Tony was asking for her."

"And…?"

"And she picked up the phone in the office, closed the door."

"And…?"

"And nothing. That was that. That's all I remember."

"Did they talk long, short? Did she raise her voice? How did she look when the call was over?"

Gino threw up his arms in surrender. "I don't know. I don't remember anything except some guy named Tony asked for Alfetta, and I told her, and she took the call in the office. That's all I remember. I don't pay attention. I'm lucky I remembered anything about it."

Stumpf wouldn't let go. "That's what I'm wondering: why do you even remember some guy named Tony called, weeks ago, and asked for Alfetta? Why would you remember that?"

Gino was getting flustered. "Because you just reminded me? I don't know, all right?"

Redding changed the subject. "Can we look, one more time, at your live videos? I just had a thought."

Gino was happy to get away from Stumpf. "Sure," and he headed to the office, the detectives in trail. "What do you want to see?"

"Just what's on here, right now," Redding said, and looked at all four shots on the screen. He could see the tip of the bumper of the car he and Stumpf had pulled up in. He and Fred exchanged a glance. "Thank you, Gino," he said.

"Is… is that all?" he asked.

"Yes. Thank you, Gino," Stumpf said, and he and Redding left through the shop and the back door, walked around to their car, making note of exactly where it parked.

Outside, Stumpf turned to the older detective. "What now?" Redding answered, "Well, Gino doesn't know anything more than he's told us. What do you think?"

"About what?"

"About any of it? About Estes, Alfetta, that Tony guy…"

Stumpf said, "I think Tony's somebody we need to talk to. Tony Gemelli. We've known about him for what—a week—and we don't know anything about him."

"Who does?"

"You mean, who's still alive? I think Alfetta might be useful. She was running away from something, and I don't think she killed her friend."

"If she's running from Tony, why would she bring us to him?"

Stumpf said, "To get him off her back, maybe?"

"She's going to implicate herself, big time, in his operation."

"Call Plessy. See what we can throw at her, then remove, bit by bit?"

Redding said, "Worth a try. By the way, whose case are we working on here?"

"Okay, you call Plessy."

Chapter Twenty–three: Tony Gemelli

"Okay, Jacob," Redding began, "Here's what we know. Here's what we believe. Here's what we need." He looked at Plessy for effect. "Now, what can we do?" He laid out the cases, with Stumpf joining at appropriate times.

After half an hour, he said, "How can we make Alfetta bring us Tony?"

Plessy looked at his notes, took a sip of his soda, stood up, walked around the room, sat down, rubbed his chin, looked at his notes again, coughed, took another sip, and drew a deep breath. He let it out slowly. "I don't know. She doctored the books in her own company, defrauded herself and her father. He could bring a civil suit. But he won't. And that's not us, anyway. She traded her own Miata for that piece of junk PT Cruiser. Crazy, but not criminal. Did she lie to you, steal any money, kill anybody?"

Stumpf said, "So, she's helping Lulita run cigarettes for Tony. Lulita holds the money, even. Alfetta's clean. Well, pretty clean. How do we make her help?"

"What kind of woman is she? I mean, could we appeal to her humanity, ask her to help?"

"She already said she'd help," Redding said, "if she got immunity. But if we don't charge her with a bunch of stuff, what's she getting immunity *from?*"

Plessy said, "What does she know, that we need? Specifically."

"She has Tony's phone number, maybe how to find him, maybe some of his trust, though she's new in his organization. I doubt he'll feel like helping her, out of the goodness of his heart. You know, if she 'asks nicely' and all."

"Does she know where Tony was stashing the cigarettes for Lulita to pick up?"

"Somewhere near here, near Michigan City, she told us," Redding said. "She didn't want to know, and Tony didn't tell her, in any event."

Connie knocked on the door. She leaned in. "Hate to interrupt, but those two stabbing victims they found in a warehouse off US 12 in Michigan City, same weekend as our Lulita Estes—LaPorte County up there just brought in a guy named Tony Gemelli. That's all I know so far. Tony Gemelli. That's your Tony, right? I thought you'd want to know." Then she left.

Redding jumped for the door. "Connie! Get us in touch with whoever's holding him! Don't let him go. He's wanted here for…" He turned to Plessy.

Plessy said, "Uh, tax evasion, transportation of large quantities of cigarettes with intent to resell, conspiracy, RICO, and… oh, what the hell— murder and conspiracy to commit murder."

Redding said, "Is that good enough?" Connie smiled, went back to her desk.

Redding looked at Stumpf, then turned to Plessy. "You sure?"

"You want him held?" Plessy nodded. "They'll hold him. I'll go work on the charges, might have to amend some of them." He smiled, tipped an imaginary hat, and left.

Stumpf looked at Redding. "So, we let Alfetta dangle until we need her, eh?"

"Or until we can come up with something she did that's more serious than running a yellow light in another state, yeah."

Half an hour later, they were at the LaPorte County lockup. Tony was sitting in an interrogation room, wrists chained to the table. He was tall and dark, and yes, handsome, looking like a cross between Julio Iglesias and a younger Dean Martin.

Forty–five years old, he wore a light tan double–breasted suit, unbuttoned, shined brown shoes, and no tie. His white shirt was open, and there was a dirt ring inside the collar of his shirt. He looked straight ahead when the detectives came in.

"Mr. Gemelli," Stumpf began. "I'm Detective Stumpf and this is Detective Redding. We're here because we heard you ran into some kind of trouble here, and we thought maybe you could help us with a little trouble we had just down the street in our jurisdiction. Have you been read your rights?"

He continued to look straight ahead. Tony said, "Lawyer."

Redding tried next. "Tony, we just drove a long way to see you. We have a case that you're not even a suspect in, but we think you can help us with it. And maybe we can help you get out of here. You understand we've come a long way?"

"Waste of gas," Tony said. But then he looked at Redding and said, "I'm not a suspect? So why am I here?"

"You're not a suspect that we're interested in," he answered. "What they've got you for here, we don't know and we don't care. But we have a dead lady on our hands, and we think you might have known her."

He looked straight at Redding. "You mean Lulita? I never met her."

Stumpf and Redding looked at each other. Stumpf said, "Yes, Lulita Estes. But why would you immediately bring her up, if you never met her? You psychic or something, Gemelli?"

"They already asked me about her. But I don't know anything about her murder. Nothing."

"We have a witness, says you two worked together."

"She's a lunatic."

"She? What makes you think our witness is a 'she?'"

"He, she, whatever," Tony said, but he knew that wouldn't work. "Yeah, 'she.' You're talking about that truck lady, right? She's a lunatic. Yeah, we worked together one time, last winter. But she didn't come through for me, so I told her I never wanted to see her again. She still owes me money."

Redding said, "She owes you money? How much?"

"A lot," he said. "Plus interest. She's crazy. I'm telling you."

"Enough so she'd be afraid of seeing you again? Enough to make her leave home without notice, take off, ditch her car? That much?"

Gemelli looked down again. "Maybe. Hard to say what crazy people going to do, they get into a jam."

"What did she owe you, Gemelli? A couple grand? Fifty? A hundred?"

"More," he said. "A lot more."

Redding continued. "And you think she had it, that she took it?"

"Obviously."

"Then why, Redding said, "would she trade her Miata for a rusty, awful PT Cruiser? Why wouldn't she just buy a car, leave the Miata at home until things blew over?"

"She traded that sweet Miata for a PT Cruiser?" Gemelli smiled. "Told you she's crazy."

"A rusty, beat–up one. So, let's say you're telling the truth about her being crazy. Why would even a crazy person do that, if she had 'a lot more than a hundred grand' on her?" Redding rested his case.

"What do you want?"

Stumpf said, "We're looking for the killer of Lulita Estes, and we're looking for somebody who's running cigarettes from Indiana to the streets of Chicago. Lulita, we believe, was driving those cigarettes to a city called Dolton, Illinois, south of Chicago, when she was killed. They found her body in the truck we believe she was driving, parked in the lot where the truck should have been rented. We have the lady who rented the trucks, your Alfetta, formerly of the Miata, in custody. She told us about you, so we want to talk with you."

"What'd she tell you?

"Enough so we're interested talk to you, skipping dinner, driving up here. And we're cranky when we haven't been fed."

Redding took up the conversation. "Look, Tony. We know about the cigarettes. We know your guys got knocked off at the warehouse. We think the same murderer may have killed Lulita Estes. If we catch that murderer, we may find out who killed your men. We may find your cigarettes. Wait—no, the FBI got your cigarettes, my bad. But we may find your money. And for all we know, some of that money may even be legitimately yours. But now we've got your two dead guys, our dead Lulita, no money, and really no suspects."

"Not even me?"

"Why would you kill off your organization and give ten pallets of cigarettes to the FBI? Or BATF, even?"

Tony sat, quiet. Redding kept going. "Those ten pallets of cigarettes—they were a lot more recent than you said. And ten pallets of cigarettes, that's maybe a quarter–million dollars. We don't believe this was your first shipment, was it, Tony? and we don't think you're stealing them—we don't have any such regular, large cigarette thefts anywhere in the whole Midwest. So, you bought them, pretty much fair and square. You were robbed, probably by whoever killed your guys and Lulita Estes. We need a little help here, is all. Find out who killed your guys, stole your money."

"Alfetta stole my money. I already told you that."

"And I told you she didn't have enough money to buy a crappy car. And when they arrested her, she only had thirteen grand with her. That's nothing, compared to what you say she stole.

Alfetta didn't steal your money." He didn't mention that she had also cleaned out the U–Drive–Em accounts.

"Who did?"

"You see, Tony, we don't know. But if we all work on this together, we may all find out."

"So I'm being held here on, what charges, exactly?"

Stumpf said, "We don't know what charges you were picked up on. As for us, you're being held under suspicion of running bootleg cigarettes out of our jurisdiction, and we take that very seriously."

"Where the hell is my lawyer?"

"You gonna work with us or not?" Stumpf, irritated and hungry. Grouchy.

"Why don't you two go get lunch, put some friendly sauce on it while you're at it, and I'll talk to my damn lawyer, and you come back in an hour and we'll talk."

Redding looked at Stumpf. He nodded. They stood up and the door opened. Redding looked back over his shoulder. "See you in a while, Tony. You be here when we get back, okay?"

"Yeah," he said. As the detectives left for dinner, Gemelli's lawyer walked into the room. Stumpf knew. He heard them exchange greetings as the door closed.

"What're we going to do if he stays clammed up?" Stumpf asked.

"Same thing we're already doing," Redding said. "Following leads, finding and looking at evidence. Talking. Listening. Praying never hurts, but I look at that as a last resort."

Stumpf raised an eyebrow.

"So, we pray tomorrow. Today, we have some lunch and think about what to do with that guy."

They slid into opposite sides of the table at the booth by the back wall, ordered—Stumpf a mushroom cheeseburger and Redding, baked chicken. Both with water, no lemon.

"He doesn't know about Lulita, does he? Not all about Lulita, I mean. Like who killed her." Stumpf said.

Redding said, "Maybe not, but he sure knows about those two dead guys in his warehouse. And I don't think he's on the up and up about that, at all."

"Do we have any information on them?"

"They were Cuban, not Mexican. Legal immigrants. The one called Ché was working on becoming a citizen. They've been working for Tony—he paid Social on them and everything—both for over four years. Doesn't explain why they worked for that smuggler."

"Doesn't explain what else Tony was doing, more like," Stumpf replied. "Do you think

Gemelli considered them more than employees? Friends, possibly? Is there something there we could use?"

"You met him, same as I did. What do you think?"

"Well, I think he hates Alfetta. Not rational. Well, maybe not rational. He won't tell us how much she cost him. She didn't steal from him; she lost his shipment. He doesn't care that there's a difference. He just sees his money gone."

Redding said, "Maybe she hijacked it, got some help."

"No, I don't think so. She and Lulita had ninety–six thousand dollars in the bank. That's not enough, if she's been stealing."

"Maybe she's not been stealing, up until this time. That truck had extra miles on it." He leaned back. "You know, Fred, maybe we've been looking at the wrong thing. This was an unusual shipment. Those extra miles point to a side trip.

"Let's assume for the moment that Lulita picked up at the regular place. That means she drove a couple extra miles beyond the usual dropoff point."

"Jerry, you're right. Why would they deliver a Johnny Lift, if they were going to the usual place? There'd already be something there. And those guys weren't professionals, like guys in any warehouse would be. They looked like Keystone Cops on that surveillance video, unloading that lift." They both laughed.

"So Fred, you're saying that shipment was hijacked, probably by the two guys we saw walk off. They're somewhere in Chicago, if they haven't hopped a train."

"But…" Fred said, "they walked off. There was still a living driver in the truck. A third guy, or… Lulita was still driving the truck. Those guys stole Tony's cigarettes, killed the guys in his warehouse, forced Lulita to drive them to the new location—who was that girl that told her boss about they only wanted the place for a day?"

"Fred, that's it. Maybe. So, they forced Lulita to divert the shipment, but then they just sent her home? Why?"

"Remember, they wanted that space until Sunday night. They had an arrangement with somebody near there, to pick everything up. They needed the truck out of there, and so they sent Lulita home. She probably didn't know about the Cubans. Wasn't scared of the new guys—maybe the Cubans even introduced the murderers as friends or co–workers. Maybe she knew them from prior shipments."

"But," Jerry said, "they were going to a new place, a place where Tony didn't send them. How the hell did Alfetta figure this out, and we couldn't?"

"We weren't looking at it. Alfetta knew, down to the tenth of a mile, how far the trip was supposed to go. This last trip was longer. She went to the original distance—she knew what city it was in—and she just added a couple miles to wherever the storage units were—it wouldn't be a closer one, and if the other ones were closer together than, say, two miles, she eliminated that pair. And then she called to see if they had ten–by–twenties. They don't all have ten–by–twenties."

"So, we can look for storage units that have ten–by–twenties, two miles closer to us. Get a warrant. Get some leverage on Tony."

Fred said, "Yes, storage units, two miles closer, that have ten–by–twenties, but none available. Tony's got one—maybe more than one—that's been rented for a while. If we want to start praying, we can pray it's rented in his name or one of his guys' names, save us a bunch of time and make the warrant easier to get."

"Okay, genius," Jerry said. "Let's go back and ask Tony if he wants to help. We've got something to negotiate with, now. First, I'll call Connie, see if she can find our storage complex." Jerry left the tip. Stumpf drove, while Jerry called Connie.

They arrived at the jail, having been gone under an hour. They had a plan, excited, if that's the word, to share it with Tony. "Who knows?" Jerry said. "Maybe our prayers are already answered."

Tony Gemelli was gone. "We couldn't hold him," the deputy said. "His lawyer walked him out ten minutes ago."

Redding looked at Stumpf. "Maybe we should be praying that Connie gets somewhere." And his phone rang. It was Connie.

"Yes… Yes… Really? He's right here… I'll tell Fred… Connie, you're wonderful," Redding said. "Thank you, Connie."

"What?" Fred Stumpf was swimming in anticipation, like a kid on Christmas Eve.

"There is only one place that would fit," Redding said. "It's called Storage King. It's two miles closer than Locked & and Safe, and…" He wanted to torture Stumpf a little more. "It has ten–by–twenties, one of which has been rented for over a year to a guy named…"

"Oh, lord, Jerry, spit it out."

"A guy named Ché Ricardo."

"What? Who the hell is Ché Ricardo?"

"Those are the first names of Tony's Cubans, the dead guys in his warehouse. Ché and Ricardo. Those are Tony's units. We're going to Chicago right now."

"By the time we get there, the judges will all have gone home to dinner. They're not going to help a couple of Hoosiers," Stumpf said.

"And Tony knows he needs to make a move before we get a warrant, and he knows we're getting close. So we go tonight and do some old–fashioned surveillance."

Stumpf said, "Great. It's been a long time since I spent a night in a car, listening to some old man snore."

"Let's go, Fred. I'll buy you a new toothbrush, and we can share the Colgate."

On the way, they called Connie, told her what they were doing, asked her to let the Dolton PD to know what they were up to and be ready, but without sharing too much detail.

Chapter Twenty–four: The bust

They parked the unmarked car on the far side of the Storage King, where one of them could see the door to the Ché Ricardo unit from the driver's seat. Stumpf walked to the office, showed the resident kid his badge but not for long enough that he could notice it was from Indiana, and explained in the vaguest terms possible why he was there, and—oh, yeah, are you open all night? If you had a gate code, you could get in.

Stumpf took up another vantage point inside the complex, raised his hand to Redding, who turned on his flasher once. They settled in, the shift until just after the gate locked going to Stumpf.

When the kid locked the place up, not quite dark yet, Redding maneuvered the car so he wouldn't be seen.

When the gate closed behind him, Stumpf went back to his spot. He was about to switch places with Redding when the gate opened and a ratty stake truck rolled in and went straight to Tony's unit. Tony followed in his car, parked in front of the truck, keeping the rear clear. Two guys jumped out of the truck; one walked around the front and helped Tony open the overhead and the other walked around the back of the truck, opening a gate and reaching in, then tossing some dirty tarps over the side, on the ground.

Tony and the other guy already had the lift in position under the first pallet as the team from the Dolton PD assembled just outside the gate, out of sight of the three men. Redding had driven to face the gate, but didn't go in. Just waited for Stumpf to walk over and open the gate from the inside.

Then Redding drove in, down a row that took him around all the units to face Tony's car; the Dolton PD's cars, three of them, followed, boxing in Tony's car and the truck.

Tony bolted past Redding before he could get out of the car, ran around the end of the row of units and behind the building. He climbed the fence and dropped down the other side, practically straight into the jaws of Hans, the PD's star K–9. He looked almost happy to see the cops and get the dog off him. Well, relieved.

"Mr. Gemelli," Redding wheezed, as he caught up and put the handcuffs on Tony, "we have to talk."

"I might be a minute," he said. "Kinda busy right now, getting arrested."

"Look, Tony, Lulita didn't steal your shipment. Your guys did."

"My guys, as you call them, are dead. You know that."

Redding moved close to Tony's face. "Look at me, Tony. Your B Team killed your A Team, took

Lulita on a ride in Alfetta's truck, with your cigarettes in it."

"And then they killed Lulita, and you want me to help find them because of that?"

"No, Tony. They didn't kill Lulita; Lulita drove the truck off after she delivered the cigarettes to a place near here. The guys killed your *guys*. That's why I thought you'd be interested in helping us, but you ran from the station, and now you're running again."

"I'm here to get my stuff. I paid for this."

"Well Tony, don't worry about your stuff. There's a team coming here to pick everything up and store it for you in a safe place, until after your trial."

Gemelli smirked. Redding continued. Stumpf had walked the long way—not jumped the fence––and he was standing behind Redding, facing Tony Gemelli. "My case is going to wrap up very soon, now that we have you and your merchandise together in time and space. But Detective Stumpf, here, he has this murder case, Lulita Estes, and he just can't get it off his mind. He's convinced your guys—your missing guys—could help fill in the timeline of her last night on Earth, and he'd like your help finding them."

Gemelli looked again at Stumpf. It was dark, but there was plenty enough light scattered around that he could see Stumpf was studying him.

Stumpf said, "Mr. Gemelli, I know this detective here," nodding at Redding, "and if you would like to help me find out more about Lulita's murder, a murder I know you didn't commit, I could put in a good word for you in whatever cases he's working up against you right now. Really—it might make you feel better. And what have you got to lose, anyway?"

"If that's an offer, I want my lawyer," Gemelli said.

"Let's talk about this with your lawyer, then. Hop into the back here; we'll give you a lift home to Indiana. You want to use one of our phones, give her a call?" He shook his head. "Not talkative this morning?"

Redding drove. Stumpf sat in the back seat with the suspect, and they left with Tony, without saying anything to the Illinois contingent. "This is going to be a mess, you know," Tony said to anyone listening. "You're in Illinois, out of your jurisdiction."

"We'll manage," said Redding, as he merged onto the highway. In a couple minutes, they had crossed into Indiana, and he and Stumpf started breathing normally, as Tony stewed.

Not far from their exit, Tony said, "So, what kind of deal are you thinking about? I mean, I didn't have anything to do with that dead lady."

Stumpf cleared his throat. "You mean killing her, or setting her up? What do you want to tell us?"

"You know damn well I didn't kill her, or want her killed, or anything like that. She was making me money." Stumpf tapped Redding's shoulder. Gemelli continued. "Hell, you know she was driving for me, using Alfetta's trucks. You still have to prove that, though. Anyway, I'll help you find those guys who did kill her—the guys who stole my cigarettes—if it'll do me enough good to make it worth my while."

"Well, Tony," Redding said over his shoulder, "we'll be able to link you to the cigarettes pretty easily. Or the feds will. The thing is, you're better off in our custody than theirs. If you want to stay in our custody, we can arrest you for complicity in Lulita Estes's murder. Then, if you want to cooperate, we'll see what we can do with the cigarette case."

"All this conversation isn't being recorded or anything, right?"

Stumpf said, "I'm not. Jerry, you?" Redding shook his head, grunted something. "Okay, Tony, let's get to work. We'll be home in ten minutes and then we'll Mirandize you for real. Start telling us what you think will help round up your guys."

At the station, they turned on the camera in the interrogation room, started recording. "Anthony

Gemelli, you are under arrest for the murder of Lulita Sharonda Estes. You have the right to remain silent…"

All Tony said was, "Lawyer," and they put him in his own cozy cell until his lawyer could again talk to the judge and get him out.

Stumpf looked at his phone. "Oh, crap," he said, ostensibly to himself, but so that Redding could hear him. "Looks like I didn't turn my phone back on."

Redding looked at his own phone, shook his head, and turned his on, as well.

Chapter Twenty–five:
Monday morning going down

When Stumpf came into the station Monday morning, Connie jumped up. "Good morning, Detective Stumpf," she said, as a mother to her wayward son. "Where were you and Detective Redding last night? I was getting calls at home from people I never heard of, saying you're a couple of kidnappers." She walked around to the front of her reception desk, reached back, picked up a scratch pad. "Here's a list of their numbers. I'd suggest you call them back soon." She smiled. "No later than right after lunch."

"Thanks, Connie. Have you seen our guest? He's back there, marking time."

"Not any more, Fred. They came at six o'clock with an order to pick him up. He's gone."

Redding walked in before Stumpf could react. Fred whirled to him. "Jerry, they picked Tony up at six this morning."

Connie broke in. "Before I got here. They came with a federal warrant, two marshals. Took him away."

"Where is he now?"

"I guess they'll get back to us. Maybe if you have a look at that list I just gave Fred, return some of the calls, you'll get your answer." Connie crossed her arms. She was through with her "boys."

Stumpf looked at the list of messages. "There's… let's see… eleven calls here, but only three numbers. You want to split these up?"

Redding shook his head, said, "Let's do these together, on speaker. Is there any room in your office?" Stumpf just looked at him, a smirk on his face. "Okay, my office. Let's get to this."

The calls were from Dolton, the BATFE, and finally from the Marshals Service.

"Let's start with Dolton," Redding said. "They've been decent about this." The call was friendly, Redding thanking them and apologizing for leaving without saying good–bye. The Dolton chief was quiet most of the time, and as the call wrapped up, finished by saying, "You owe me a big one."

Redding said thanks for all the help and for understanding, "and you can keep the cigarettes, if you like."

"Yeah, thanks. But I mean it—you owe me."

"Fred broke in. Yes, Chief, we do realize that. Thanks again."

The call to ATF wasn't as pleasant, but it was shorter, since it was just a cussing–out by the fed and a threat for the future. He reminded Stumpf and Redding that he had a long memory and the next time, it wouldn't be just Marshals he'd send. Blah, blah, blah… etcetera.

Jerry and Fred looked at each other, nearly laughing, and Fred apologized for causing the poor man so much trouble.

The Marshals Service were professional and didn't get involved, said they couldn't disclose where they had taken Gemelli, that they'd be told in due time and that it was now a federal case and they'd have to wait in line for him.

Stumpf said, "Jerry, that wasn't near as bad as I thought it would be."

And Jerry said, "We haven't seen our own Chief yet."

Stumpf said, "What's our story?"

"Just the truth. That's it's over, there's no paperwork. He'll be fine with that. Tony's somebody else's problem now; we're going back to work on your case."

"What's wrong with *your* case?"

"Fred, they have Tony. They have their cigarettes. They're dealing with Dolton from now on, whatever's left to mop up. My case has been taken out of play. So, let's see what we can do to find our Lulita's killer."

Stumpf went to his office and was back in a couple minutes with his case folder and two coffees, one of which had spilled on his hand, his shirt, and the folder. Redding grabbed a tissue and cleaned up the folder first, put it on his desk. "So, Tony's guys that we want to talk to came here via Chicago. And they stayed at the relo center. I'll bet they met somebody there. And the Center will have ID photos. We'll find 'em." Stumpf continued, "So, which part of this d'you want?"

Giovanni Aguilar and Galena Flores were in the system only a couple months, so their records had current photographs. Their faces were soon famous all over Chicago media, extending naturally into northwest Indiana, and police across the Midwest were on high alert for them.

It was a burned–out license plate light on a stolen Taurus on I–55 heading for St. Louis that got the Salvadorans stopped on Monday night.Tuesday morning, they were back in LaPorte County, Indiana.

After the city, county, and state were finished asking them questions, Fred and Jerry were invited. By this time, their guilt in the murders and their part in hijacking Lulita's truck had been established. Not beyond a reasonable doubt as in court, but good enough for government work.

They knew they were likely to become permanent residents of the United States of America, their lack of documentation notwithstanding.

Stumpf and Redding didn't have a lot of time; FBI and BATFE were on the way. Fred Stumpf started. The tired interpreter sat on standby.

Their equally–tired lawyer pretended to be interested, his head nodding now and then.

"So, how did you get Lulita to drive you to Illinois?" Stumpf asked, easy question first.

Gio answered. "We tol' her Tony wants us to ride along this time. Was easy 'til we get to the regular place."

Galena offered, "Then we tell her we know all about her. She tell us all about her home life, her girls, where she live. She like to talk. So she had to go where we told her."

"Did you have to hurt her?" Stumpf asked, giving them the easy way out.

"No, no. She was fine. She was scare, is all," Gio said. "We tol' her, stay in the truck. She stay in the truck. We ask her if she need directions to the highway, but she say 'no.' She drive away, she is fine. We din' do nothing to her." He added, for no particular reason, "She was a nice lady."

Galena smiled and nodded, realizing that they weren't getting into additional trouble.

"What time was that?"

"That was maybe eleven. I din' look. Did you?" He looked at Galena, who shook his head. "Not midnight. Not too late."

Stumpf turned to Redding. "Anything you want to ask these guys?"

Redding shook his head. Then he said, "Thank you, both of you. Your cooperation will be noted." And the detectives left.

Chapter Twenty–six:
the daughters Estes

Walking to the car, Stumpf turned to Redding. "Jerry, it's gotta be Daniel Estes."

"Let's get the family in again," Redding said. "Both girls. We can question them separately, Estes and the daughter. You talk to Sharonda and Lilly. The older girl seems to have a liking for you. Haven't a clue why, but hey. Meantime, I'll be putting the heat on Daniel. But I think you'll get more out of Sharonda than I will out of Estes. She wants to tell you more, I think. Maybe her memory has gotten better."

"I agree," Stumpf said. "She was really polite with me. Teenagers are never polite. Definitely up to something, throwing her dad off. She probably thinks I'll believe she's always like that."

"Did you have enough time with her at school?"

"Oh, hell, no. By the time I got to see her, it was almost time for her to go. And those biddies, standing on the other side of the glass, practically with their noses making marks. Even if we had time, they would have been intimidating."

"So, we bring in Estes and the girls," Redding said. "Make it like we're questioning him. You 'babysit' the girls and find out as much as you can. We're running low on suspects, but the husband— whatever his motive—he's still standing."

Estes was annoyed, and showed it. "It's great to give the folks a day off," he said, "but I don't like pulling Sharonda out of school. She's just getting started."

Stumpf said, "Thanks for coming in, Mr. Estes. I know it's tough on all of you, missing work, missing school. But we're closing in on your wife's killer. You know we caught up with the two men who we believe hijacked her truck?"

Estes stepped back, surprised. He smiled. "That's great news. Really great. Did they confess yet?"

"Well, no, they didn't," Stumpf continued. "But we maybe got some good information from them. We just want to double–check what they told us with what you know. Detective Redding has been on their case; he'll talk with you. But it's best if you're in private. Mind if I entertain your girls while you two are talking?"

"That would be great," Estes said.

Redding said, "They'll be in the break room. We can use my office to talk. It's private." He motioned, but Estes was familiar with the uncomplicated floor plan. Stumpf led Sharonda, holding Lilly's hand, into the break room.

"Mind if I record?" Redding asked. "It'll be easier than writing everything down. I'll still use this," he said, setting a yellow pad on the desk as he dusted off his jacket and hung it up, "but an audio will help me fill in any blanks or things I can't read later." He laughed. "Oh," as if it was an afterthought, after he turned on the recorder, "do you want your lawyer present?"

"I don't need a lawyer," Estes said, smiling and at ease. "I just want to help you find whoever killed Luli."

They sat down, Redding on his side of the desk, Estes opposite.

"Okay, Mr. Estes," he said, "I know we've gone over most of this before, but bear with me one more time."

In the break room, Sharonda had sat Lilly down on the table, facing them, soft drinks at a safe distance. Lilly slept all the way from Dolton, so she was alert when Stumpf began. "It's such a pleasure to see you again, Miss Sharonda."

"And you as well, Detective Stump."

He let it go. "Pleasant weather we're having, isn't it?" He put a piece of paper next to Lilly, gave her a blue crayon.

"Indeed." Then she dropped the façade, her expression serious. "We didn't finish talking about Mom."

"We have plenty of time now. Nobody's watching us and your dad's busy answering his own questions. Let's bring me up to date. Tell me again: you woke up, you heard your mom. You're still sure?"

"I'm positive. I know I wasn't dreaming. I know I heard them talking, I mean whispering, by the front door. That was the night she…"

"Yes. Sorry to put you through this again. You couldn't hear what they said? Not a single word?"

"No, just sort of laughing, Then it was quiet and I went back to sleep."

"Did you get out of bed?"

"No, I was tired. I stayed in bed. But I was totally awake for that, I swear."

Lilly shifted, nearly kicked over Stumpf's drink. "Me," she said.

Sharonda looked at her, said sharply, "Lilly, be quiet. We're talking."

"Me," she said again. "I was up."

They snapped to attention. Stumpf put his hand in front of Sharonda; he'll handle this. "You were up?" he said.

"Yes," the tiny girl said. "When Mommy never came back that night."

"But it was late," Fred said, leaning back a little, to give the toddler some room. "Shouldn't you be in bed?"

"I was up," she repeated. "Augie bark. I was up." She paused a moment, perhaps building drama on purpose. Whether intentional or not, it worked. Then she spoke. "I saw Mommy and Daddy at the door."

Sharonda was turning pale, clutching her knees under the table.

Stumpf tried to be avuncular. "What did they say?"

Lilly said, "Something grown up. Then Mommy, her phone ringed and Daddy push her head down to see it and Mommy went to sleep."

"What did your Daddy do?" Stumpf was shaking, but she couldn't comprehend that. Sharonda saw it; she was shaking, too.

"Daddy took Mommy away."

"You mean, to beddy–bye?"

"Outside away."

Stumpf was thinking of a way to follow up. "Did Mommy come back in the morning?"

"No, Daddy. Just Daddy." Then she stopped for a moment. "When is Mommy coming home?"

Sharonda broke into tears. Stumpf took his eyes off the little girl on the table, looked at Sharonda. She was crying tears of disbelief, grief, maybe… anger? "Augie barked! Later, though. I remember. It was like four in the morning. He never barks then." Emotions coursed across her face. Then, *"I hate him!"* she yelled.

Anger, definitely anger.

Stumpf started to say something, but gave up on that as she ran past him. "Sharonda, stop!" but she was already out the door by the time he got up.

She ran next door and threw open Redding's door, started pounding on her father, tears pouring down her face, the spit coming out of her mouth as she screamed, *"You killed Mom! You killed her! I hate you! I hate you!"*

Daniel instinctively pushed his daughter away as Stumpf grabbed her elbows and pulled her back. "I *hate* you!" she screamed, as Stumpf pulled her into the hallway and Redding closed and locked his door.

Sharonda's rage abated. Spent, she sobbed, embraced Stumpf, his arms limp at his sides, as Connie approached.

"Sharonda, it's me, Connie." Sharonda looked at her, whimpered, walked to Connie's extended hands, took them, started to sob. "Come with me, Sharonda; let's get you cleaned up."

And there was a thud and a scream from the break room. Lilly had scooched off the table, aimed for the chair, and missed. She was lying on the floor, crying.

Sharonda let go of Connie's hands and ran to her sister. "Oh, Lilly, Lilly, Lilly!"

Lilly stopped crying. Sharonda said, "Lilly fall down. Boom!"

And the little girl smiled and said, "Boom!" and she laughed, started to cry again, then decided to laugh.

And Sharonda laughed. She leaned over her sister and said, "Don't tell Daddy, okay?" And Lilly held out her hand. The two sisters, for the first time with an audience, exchanged a pinkie–swear.

Daniel burst out of the room, gathered up Lilly, looked at everybody else. He winced as he saw the hate in Sharonda's eyes. He got no sympathy from any of the other three, either, nor from the two uniforms who stood between him and the door.

—— THE END ——

Epilogue

Josh Terwilliger had an uneventful trip to Texas, where he worked on The Wall, then started a home remodeling business, and married a retired dancer named Felina, who had moved to Socorro after a sad experience at the cantina in El Paso, where she worked until a few months before.

Daniel Estes pleaded guilty to involuntary manslaughter in Illinois and was found guilty on several lesser charges. He was sentenced to nine years in the Illinois State Prison in Joliet.

When Sharonda went home the night Daniel was arrested, Gumpy and Nana were there, and did their best to comfort her, but she stayed angry. When the old folks went to bed, Sharonda broke into Daniel's nightstand and found the rolls of gold coins and a large pistol, plus a box of ammunition. She hid them, never telling anybody until her first wedding anniversary, when she told her husband about half the gold coins. And when Lilly got married, Sharonda and her husband astounded the new couple with five gold pieces.

Fingerprint evidence from the license plate was too badly degraded to play as evidence against the Salvadorans, but other evidence gathered in LaPorte County against Aguilar and

Flores helped convict them both of murder in
Indiana; they were then extradited to El Salvador
where they faced myriad charges. Flores died
under sketchy circumstances in prison a year
later; Aguilar could be released from prison there
in as few as eleven more years. He may yet be
repatriated to the United States to face his
sentence for murder, though there is no interest
among Indiana law enforcement to see him again.

Alfetta Tonelli was convicted for the federal
crime of transporting the cigarettes interstate to
avoid payment of taxes. Later, her father, Vittorio,
sued her for embezzling the company's funds.

Vittorio, less than a year after he successfully
sued Alfetta, died in his sleep, his body discovered
by his home health worker, who called 911 half
an hour after she arrived.

Gino was surprised to learn that he had
inherited the U–Drive–Em franchise from his
mentor and friend, Vittorio Tonelli. He kept Eli
on, eventually appointing him manager of
Sabbatini's second franchise.

Sharonda and Lilly were raised by their
grandparents. Sharonda buckled down and
became an A student, was voted "Most Likely to

Lead" in her graduating class and went on to earn a scholarship to study Criminal Justice at the University of Chicago.

Gumpa and Nana died within two months of each other during Sharonda's senior year.

Sharonda continued to live with her sister in the same house the remaining months until graduation, when, as she said, "the executor finally got around to selling it." She and ten–year–old Lilly moved to Chicago, where Sharonda began her career in the Records Department of the Cook County Police.

Tony Gemelli was convicted on over a dozen counts relating to smuggling, interfering with police, lying to various Law Enforcement officers, and nine counts of perjury and suborning perjury. He was sentenced to serve concurrent sentences totaling twenty–two years in four federal and state institutions, where he continues to build his network and plan his race for Mayor of Chicago.

Connie Clark received a two–pound box of chocolates with no indication of the source except a note that said, "Thank you, you luscious dame." Stumpf denied any knowledge.

Augie ran away, just bolted, about a week after Lulita's murder. That weekend, Nana and Gumpy and the girls went to visit Lulita's grave, and from the parking lot, Sharonda saw the dog, stretched over the grave. He wasn't moving, and he didn't, even as Sharonda knelt next to him. She was crying as she stood up, brushed against Augie's motionless front paw. And the dog opened his eyes, lifted his head… and went home with his family.

About Tim Kern

The author is best known as an aviation writer, with bylined features in over fifty aviation publications worldwide. Unlike his usual fare, however, this book contains no verifiable facts, and the people and their quotes are all made up.

Kern taught economics for fifteen years, to students from high school through postgraduate levels.

His nine–year radio show, *Tim Kern, Talking Sense,* aired on over 200 stations. He has raced motorcycles and still rides regularly; he's a former car racer and race instructor, and he was a professional mechanic on a championship–winning Can–Am team. He holds a Private Pilot certificate.

He has other published titles, including his first book, The Executive Primer (serialized over three years in SUCCESS Magazine). His crime novels, published by Mystery One™ Publishing, represent a new venture.

Other Book Titles by Tim Kern

<u>Non–fiction, how–to:</u>
The Executive Primer
The Manual by Eduardo
The Americans' Fight to Survive (co–author; credited as editor)
Note: the above works are out of print.

<u>Fiction:</u>
EGOFALL: Ego. Paranoia. Murder
Caught by a Cat: Not a childrens' book
Like Murder Like Son

To receive advance notice of new books and occasional free short stories by Tim Kern, send an email with "FUTURE WORKS" as the subject to INFO@TIMKERN.COM

Connect with Tim Kern

If you enjoyed this book, please take the time to write a review, and by all means, tell others (and naturally if you didn't, please don't).

There are a few ways to get in touch with the author.
His Facebook page, Writings of Tim Kern, is one such method.
[https://www.facebook.com/TimKernWritings/]

His URL is usually reliable.
www.TimKern.com

Tim is available for speaking engagements and book signings.

Direct email is another method.
And at the risk of sounding redundant, to get on Tim Kern's email list (and receive periodic free short stories and articles, questions, and advance notice of upcoming publications),
send an email request to
info@timkern.com

*Please remember to leave a review of my book at your favorite retailer
or on my Facebook page.
Thank you.*

www.ingramcontent.com/pod-product-compliance
Lightning Source LLC
Chambersburg PA
CBHW021412110726
47901CB00008B/2149